THE STUNNED REACTION . . .

"Mr. Trumbo sets this story down almost without pause or punctuation and with a fury amounting to eloquence."

—The New York Times

"[It is] very hard to write about **Johnny Got His Gun** without being guilty of understatement or hysterics. It is a terrifying book, of an extraordinary emotional intensity."

—Washington Post

"An extraordinarily agitating book, passionate in its language, potent in its emotional effect, a novel that tells in unsparingly honest words what a wickedly gruesome business war is, and how wickedly wasteful. **Johnny Got His Gun**, full of horror and hurt, will be a terrific and vivid experience for anyone who reads it."

—Boston Herald

"It is hard to imagine a more persuasive argument for staying out of war than this smooth, savage, brilliant tale."

—Chicago Daily News

AND FROM EUROPE

"Only people who do not fear the truth will be able to read this book. It is the most horrifying accusation against war that has ever been written in our alphabet . . ."

—Der Mittag

"To all those who still have a good opinion of war, this book is directed."

—Forum Academicum

"For us Germans, [the book] has either been withheld by design, or the mentality of our publishers is such that they thought it wiser to keep silent about the book . . . All other anti-war books I know pale beside it . . ."

—Die Tat

"This is the most horrifying, moving protest which has ever been raised against war . . . Because Trumbo restricts himself to this individual case and ignores the actual noise of battle and all the obvious aspects of war itself, because he refuses to make any attempt at conveying an atmosphere but tells his tale simply, almost soberly and yet impressively, he achieves the highest effects."

—National Zeitung

johnny got his gun
dalton
trumbo

BANTAM BOOKS · LONDON · TORONTO · NEW YORK

This low-priced Bantam Book
has been completely reset in a type face
designed for easy reading, and printed
from new plates. It contains the complete
text of the original hard-cover edition.
NOT ONE WORD HAS BEEN OMITTED.

JOHNNY GOT HIS GUN
*A Bantam Book / published by arrangement with
Lyle Stuart, Inc.*

PRINTING HISTORY
Lippincott edition published September 1939
Seven printings
Monogram publishers edition published 1946
The Liberty Book Club edition published 1952
Lyle Stuart edition published May 1959
Nine printings
Bantam edition / March 1967
New Bantam edition / March 1970
29 printings through July 1978

ISBN 0-553-12248-7

Published simultaneously in the United States and Canada

*Bantam Books are published by Bantam Books, Inc. Its trade-
mark, consisting of the words "Bantam Books" and the por-
trayal of a bantam, is registered in the United States Patent
Office and in other countries. Marca Registrada. Bantam
Books, Inc., 666 Fifth Avenue, New York, New York 10019.*

PRINTED IN THE UNITED STATES OF AMERICA

Introduction

World War I began like a summer festival—all billowing skirts and golden epaulets. Millions upon millions cheered from the sidewalks while plumed imperial highnesses, serenities, field marshals and other such fools paraded through the capital cities of Europe at the head of their shining legions.

It was a season of generosity; a time for boasts, bands, poems, songs, innocent prayers. It was an August made palpitant and breathless by the prenuptial nights of young gentlemen-officers and the girls they left permanently behind them. One of the Highland regiments went over the top in its first battle behind forty kilted bagpipers, skirling away for all they were worth—at machine guns.

Nine million corpses later, when the bands stopped and the serenities started running, the wail of bagpipes would never again sound quite the same. It was the last of the romantic wars; and *Johnny Got His Gun* was probably the last American novel written about it before an entirely different affair called World War II got under way.

The book has a weird political history. Written in 1938 when pacifism was anathema to the American left and most of the center, it went to the printers in the spring of 1939 and was published on September third—ten days after the Nazi-Soviet pact, two days after the start of World War II.

Shortly thereafter, on the recommendation of Mr. Joseph Wharton Lippincott (who felt it would stimulate sales), serial rights were sold to *The Daily Worker* of New York City. For months thereafter the book was a rally point for the left.

After Pearl Harbor its subject matter seemed as inappropriate to the times as the shriek of bagpipes. Mr. Paul Blanshard, speaking of army censorship in *The Right to Read* (1955) says, "A few pro-Axis foreign-language magazines had been banned, as well as three books, including Dalton Trumbo's pacifist novel *Johnny Get Your Gun,* produced during the period of the Hitler-Stalin pact."

Since Mr. Blanshard fell into what I hope was unconscious error both as to the period of the book's "production" and the title under which it was "produced," I can't place too much faith in his story of its suppression. Certainly I was not informed of it; I received a number of letters from service men overseas who had read it through Army libraries; and, in 1945, I myself ran across a copy in Okinawa while fighting was still in progress.

If, however, it had been banned and I had known about it, I doubt that I should have protested very loudly. There are times when it may be needful for certain private rights to give way to the requirements of a larger public good. I know that's a dangerous thought, and I shouldn't wish to carry it too far, but World War II was *not* a romantic war.

As the conflict deepened, and *Johnny* went out of print altogether, its unavailability became a civil liberties issue with the extreme American right. Peace organizations and "Mothers' " groups from all over the country showered me with fiercely sympathetic letters denouncing Jews, Communists, New Dealers and international bankers, who had suppressed my novel to intimidate millions of true Americans who demanded an immediate negotiated peace.

My correspondents, a number of whom used elegant stationery and sported tidewater addresses, maintained a network of communications that extended to the detention camps of pro-Nazi internees. They pushed the price of the book above six dollars for a used copy, which displeased me for a number of reasons, one of them fiscal. They proposed a national rally for peace-now, with me as cheer leader; they promised (and delivered) a letter campaign to pressure the publisher for a fresh edition.

Nothing could have convinced me so quickly that *Johnny* was exactly the sort of book that shouldn't be reprinted until the war was at an end. The publishers agreed. At the insistence of friends who felt my correspondents' efforts could adversely affect the war effort, I foolishly reported their activities to the F. B. I. But when a beautifully matched pair of investigators arrived at my house, their interest lay not in the letters but in me. I have the feeling that it still does, and it serves me right.

After 1945, those two or three new editions which appeared found favor with the general left, and apparently were completely ignored by everybody else, including all those passionate war-time mothers. It was out of print again during the Korean War, at which time I purchased the plates rather than have them sold to the government for conversion into munitions. And there the story ends, or begins.

Reading it once more after so many years, I've

had to resist a nervous itch to touch it up here, to change it there, to clarify, correct, elaborate, cut. After all, the book is twenty years younger than I, and I have changed so much, and it hasn't. Or has it?

Is it possible for anything to resist change, even a mere commodity that can be bought, buried, banned, damned, praised, or ignored for all the wrong reasons? Probably not. *Johnny* held a different meaning for three different wars. Its present meaning is what each reader conceives it to be, and each reader is gloriously different from every other reader, and each is also changing.

I've let it remain as it was to see what it is.

DALTON TRUMBO

Los Angeles
March 25, 1959

Addendum: 1970

Eleven years later. Numbers have dehumanized us. Over breakfast coffee we read of 40,000 American dead in Vietnam. Instead of vomiting, we reach for the toast. Our morning rush through crowded streets is not to cry murder but to hit that trough before somebody else gobbles our share.

An equation: 40,000 dead young men = 3,000 tons of bone and flesh, 124,000 pounds of brain matter, 50,000 gallons of blood, 1,840,000 years of life that will never be lived, 100,000 children who will never be born. (The last we can afford: there are too many starving children in the world already.)

Do we scream in the night when it touches our dreams? No. We don't dream about it because we don't think about it; we don't think about it because we don't care about it. We are much more interested in law and order, so that American streets may be made safe while we transform those of Vietnam into flowing sewers of blood which we replenish each year by forcing our sons to choose between a prison cell here or a coffin there. "Every time I look at the flag, my eyes fill with tears." Mine too.

If the dead mean nothing to us (except on Memorial Day weekend when the national freeway is clotted with surfers, swimmers, skiers, picnickers, campers, hunters, fishers, footballers, beer-busters), what of our 300,000 wounded? Does anyone know where they are? How they feel? How many arms, legs, ears, noses, mouths, faces, penises they've lost? How many are deaf or dumb or blind or all three? How many are single or double or triple or quadruple amputees? How many will remain immobile for the rest of their days? How many hang on as decerebrated vegetables quietly breathing their lives away in small, dark, secret rooms?

Write the Army, the Air Force, the Navy, the Marine Corps, the Army and Navy Hospitals, the Director of Medical Sciences at the National Library of Medicine, the Veterans Administration, the Office of the Surgeon General—and be surprised by what you don't learn. One agency reports 726 admissions "for amputation services" since January, 1965. Another reports 3,011 amputees since the beginning of the fiscal year 1968. The rest is silence.

The *Annual Report of the Surgeon General:*

Medical Statistics of the United States Army ceased publication in 1954. The Library of Congress reports that the Army Office of the Surgeon General for Medical Statistics "does not have figures on single or multiple amputees." Either the government doesn't think them important or, in the words of a researcher for one of the national television networks, "the military itself, while sure of how many tons of bombs it has dropped, is unsure of how many legs and arms its men have lost."

If there are no concrete figures, at least we are beginning to get comparative ones. Proportionately, Vietnam has given us eight times as many paralytics as World War II, three times as many totally disabled, 35% more amputees. Senator Cranston of California concludes that out of every hundred army veterans receiving compensation for wounds received in action in Vietnam, 12.4% are totally disabled. Totally.

But exactly how many hundreds or thousands of the dead-while-living does *that* give us? We don't know. We don't ask. We turn away from them; we avert the eyes, ears, nose, mouth, face. "Why should I look, it wasn't my fault, was it?" It was, of course, but no matter. Time presses. Death waits even for us. We have a dream to pursue, the whitest white hope of them all, and we must follow and find it before the light fails.

So long, losers. God bless. Take care. We'll be seeing you.

DALTON TRUMBO

Los Angeles
January 3, 1970

BOOK I

The Dead

i

He wished the phone would stop ringing. It was bad enough to be sick let alone having a phone ring all night long. Boy was he sick. Not from any of their sour french wine either. A man couldn't hold enough of it to get a head this big. His stomach was going round and round and round. Fine thing nobody'd answer that phone. It sounded like it was ringing in a room about a million miles wide. His head was a million miles wide too. The hell with the telephone.

That damn bell must be at the other end of the world. He would have to walk for a couple years to get to it. Ring ring ring all night long. Maybe somebody wanted something bad. Telephones ringing at night are important. You'd think they'd pay attention to it. How could they expect him to answer it anyhow? He was tired and his head was plenty big. You could stick a whole phone in his ear and he couldn't even feel it. He must have been drinking dynamite.

3

Why didn't somebody answer that goddam telephone?

"Hey Joe. Front and center."

Here he was sick as hell and like a damned fool making his way through the night shipping room toward the telephone. It was so noisy you wouldn't think anybody could hear a tiny sound like a phone ringing. Yet he had. He'd heard it above the click-click-click of the Battle Creek wrappers and the rattle of the belt conveyors and the howl of the rotary ovens upstairs and the rumble of steel route bins being hauled into place and the sputter of motors in the garage being tuned up against the morning's work and the scream of dollies that needed oil why the hell didn't somebody oil them?

He walked down the middle aisle between the steel bins that were being filled with bread. He threaded his way through the floor litter of dollies and boxes and rumpled cartons and crippled loaves. The boys looked at him as he went. He remembered their faces floating by him as he moved toward the telephone. Dutch and Little Dutch and Whitey who took shots in his spine and Pablo and Rudy and all the boys. They looked at him curiously as he passed them. Maybe that was because he was scared inside and showed it outside. He got to the phone.

"Hello."

"Hello son. Come on home now."

"All right mother I'll be right there."

He went into the lean-to office with the wide glass front where Jody Simmons the night foreman kept a close watch on his crew.

"Jody I got to go home. My father just died."

"Died? Gosh kid that's too bad. Sure kid you run

4

along. Rudy. Hey Rudy. Grab a truck and drive Joe home. His old—his father just died. Sure kid go on home. I'll have one of the boys punch you out. That's tough kid. Go home."

Rudy stepped on it. It was raining outside because it was December and Los Angeles just before christmas. The tires sizzled against the wet pavement as they went. It was the quietest night he had ever heard except for the tires sizzling and the clatter of the Ford echoing between deserted buildings in an empty street. Rudy sure stepped on it. There was a rattle somewhere back of them in the truck body that kept the same time no matter how fast they went. Rudy didn't say anything. He just drove. Way out Figueroa past big old houses and then smaller houses and then on out some more to the south end. Rudy stopped the car.

"Thanks Rudy, I'll let you know when everything's finished. I'll be back to work in a couple days."

"Sure Joe. That's all right. It's tough. I'm sorry goodnight."

The Ford grabbed for traction. Then its motor roared and it went sideslipping down the street. Water bubbled along the curb. The rain pattered down steadily. He stood there for a moment to take a good breath and then he started for the place.

The place was on the alley above a garage behind a two story house. To get to it he walked down a narrow driveway which was between two houses close together. It was black between the houses. Rain from the two roofs met there and spattered down into wide puddles with a queer wet echo like water being poured into a cistern. His feet squshed in the water as he went.

5

When he got out from between the two houses he saw lights on over the garage. He opened the door. A rush of hot air swept over him. It was hot air perfumed with the soap and scented rubbing alcohol they used for bathing his father and with the powder they put on him afterward to fight off bedsores. Everything was very quiet. He tip-toed upstairs his wet shoes still squshing a little.

In the living room his father lay dead with a sheet pulled over his face. He had been sick a long while and they had kept him in the living room because the glassed-in porch which was the bedroom for his father and mother and sisters was too drafty.

He walked over to his mother and touched her shoulder. She wasn't crying very hard.

"Did you call someone?"

"Yes they'll be here anytime. I wanted you to be here first."

His younger sister was still asleep on the glassed-in porch but his older sister only thirteen was crumpled in a corner in her bathrobe catching her breath and sobbing quietly. He looked over at her. She was crying like a woman. He hadn't realized before that she was practically grown up. She had been growing up all the time and he hadn't noticed till now when she was crying because her father was dead.

A knock came on the door downstairs.

"It's them. Let's go into the kitchen. It'll be better."

They had a little trouble getting his sister into the kitchen but she came quietly enough. It seemed she couldn't walk. Her face was blank. Her eyes were big and she was gasping more than crying. His mother sat on a stool in the kitchen and took his sister into her arms. Then he went to the head of the stairs and called down quietly.

"Come in."

Two men in gleaming clean collars opened the door down there and started up the stairs. They carried a long wicker basket. Quickly he stepped into the living room and pulled aside the sheets to have a look at his father before they reached the top of the stairs.

He looked down at a tired face that was only fifty-one years old. He looked down and thought dad I feel lots older than you. I was sorry for you dad. Things weren't going well and they never would have gone well for you and it's just as good you're dead. People've got to be quicker and harder these days than you were dad. Goodnight and good-dreams. I won't forget you and I'm not as sorry for you today as I was yesterday. I loved you dad goodnight.

They came into the room. He turned and walked into the kitchen to his mother and sister. The other sister who was only seven still slept.

There were sounds from the front room. The men's footsteps as they tip-toed around the bed. A faint woosh of covers being thrown toward the foot. Then a sound of bedsprings relaxing after eight months' use. Then a sound of wicker squeaking as it took up the burden the bed had left off with. Then after a heavy squeaking from all parts of the basket a shuffling of feet moving out of the front room and down the stairs. He wondered if they were carrying the basket evenly down the stairs or if the head was lower than the feet or if it was in any way uncomfortable. His father performing the same task would have carried the basket very gently.

When the door at the foot of the stairs closed behind them his mother began to shake a little. Her voice came like dry air.

"That's not Bill. It may seem like it but it's not."

He patted his mother's shoulder. His sister relaxed down on the floor again.

That was all.

Well why couldn't it be all then? How many times was he going to have to go through it? It was all over and finished and why couldn't the goddam phone ever stop ringing? He was nutty because he had a hangover a big hangover and he was having bad dreams. Pretty soon if he had to he'd wake up and answer the phone but somebody should do it for him if they had any consideration at all because he was tired and sick of it.

Things were getting floaty and sickly. Things were so quiet. Things were so goddam still. A hangover headache thumps and clatters and raises hell inside your skull. But this wasn't any hangover. He was a sick man. He was a sick man and he was remembering things. Like coming out of ether. But you'd think the telephone would stop ringing sometime. It couldn't just go on forever. He couldn't go over and over the same business of answering it and hearing his father was dead and then going home through a rainy night. He'd catch cold if he did that much more. Besides his father could only die once.

The telephone bell was just part of a dream. It had sounded different from any other telephone bell or any other sound because it had meant death. After all that bell was a particular kind of thing a very particular kind of thing as old Prof Eldridge used to say in Senior English. And a particular kind of thing sticks with you but there's no use of it sticking too close. That bell and its message and everything about it was way back in time and he was finished with it.

The bell was ringing again. Way far off as if echoing through a lot of shutters in his mind he could hear it. He felt as if he were tied down and couldn't answer it yet he felt as if he had to answer it. The bell sounded as lonesome as Christ ringing out in the bottom of his mind waiting for an answer. And they couldn't make connections. With each ring it seemed to get lonesomer. With each ring he got more scared.

He drifted again. He was hurt. He was bad hurt. The bell was fading. He was dreaming. He wasn't dreaming. He was awake even though he couldn't see. He was awake even though he couldn't hear a thing except a telephone that really wasn't ringing. He was mighty scared.

He remembered how when he was a kid he read The Last Days of Pompeii and awakened in the middle of a dark night crying in terror with his face suffocating in the pillow and thinking that the top of one of his Colorado mountains had blown off and that the covers were lava and that he was entombed while yet alive and that he would lie there dying forever. He had that same gasping feeling now. He had that same cowardly griping in his bowels. He was unchristly scared so he gathered his strength and made like a man buried in loose earth clawing out with his hands toward air.

Then he sickened and choked and fainted half

9

away and was dragged back by pain. It was all over his body like electricity. It seemed to shake him hard and then throw him back against the bed exhausted and completely quiet. He lay there feeling the sweat pour out of his skin. Then he felt something else. He felt hot damp skin all over him and the dampness enabled him to feel his bandages. He was wrapped in them from top to bottom. Even his head.

He really was hurt then.

The shock caused his heart to smash against his ribs. He grew prickly all over. His heart was pounding away in his chest but he couldn't hear the pulse in his ear.

Oh god then he was deaf. Where did they get that stuff about bombproof dugouts when a man in one of them could be hit so hard that the whole complicated business of his ears could be blown away leaving him deaf so deaf he couldn't hear his own heart beat? He had been hit and he had been hit bad and now he was deaf. Not just a little deaf. Not just halfway deaf. He was stone deaf.

He lay there for a while with the pain ebbing and thinking this will give me something to chew on all right all right. What about the rest of the guys? Maybe they didn't come out so lucky. There were some good boys down in that hole. How'll it seem being deaf and shouting at people? You write things on paper. No that's wrong they write things on paper to you. It isn't anything to kick up your heels and dance about but it might be worse. Only when you're deaf you're lonesome. You're godforsaken.

So he'd never hear again. Well there were a hell of a lot of things he didn't want to hear again. He never wanted to hear the biting little castanet sound

10

of a machine gun or the high whistle of a .75 coming down fast or the slow thunder as it hit or the whine of an airplane overhead or the yells of a guy trying to explain to somebody that he's got a bullet in his belly and that his breakfast is coming out through the front of him and why won't somebody stop going forward and give him a hand only nobody can hear him they're so scared themselves. The hell with it.

Things were going in and out of focus. It was like looking into one of those magnified shaving mirrors and then moving it toward you and away from you. He was sick and probably out of his head and he was badly hurt and he was lonesome deaf but he was also alive and he could still hear far away and sharp the sound of a telephone bell.

He was sinking and rising and then going in lazy quiet black circles. Everything was alive with sound. He was nuts all right. He caught a glimpse of the big ditch where he and the guys used to go swimming in Colorado before he came to Los Angeles before he came to the bakery. He could hear the splash of water as Art did one of his high dives he's a fool for diving so far why can't the rest of us do it? He looked out across the rolling meadows of Grand Mesa eleven thousand feet in the sky and saw acres of columbines stirring in a cool August breeze and heard far off the roar of mountain streams. He saw his father pulling a sled with his mother on it one Christmas morning. He heard the fresh snow squealing under the runners of the sled. The sled was his Christmas present and his mother was laughing like a girl and his dad was grinning in his slow wrinkly way.

11

They seemed to have a good time his mother and his father. Especially then. They used to flirt with each other right in front of him before the girls were born. Do you remember this? Do you remember that? I cried. You talked like this. You wore your hair so. You picked me up and I remembered how strong you were and you put me on old Frank because he was gentle and after that we rode across the river on the ice with old Frank picking his way carefully like a dog.

You remember the telephone when you were courting me? I remember everything when I was courting you even the gander that used to rush and hiss at me when I took you in my arms. You remember the telephone when you were courting me silly? I remember. Then you remember the party line going eighteen miles along Cole Creek Valley and only five customers? I remember I remember the way you looked with your big eyes and your smooth forehead you haven't changed. You remember the telephone line and how new it was? Oh it was lonely out there with nobody in three or four miles and nobody really in the world but you. And me waiting for the telephone to ring. It rang two times for us remember? Two rings and you were calling from the grocery store when the store was closed. And the receivers all along the line all five of them going click-click Bill is calling Macia click-click-click. And then your voice how funny it was to hear your voice the first time over a telephone how wonderful it always was.

"Hello Macia."

"Hello Bill how are you?"

"I'm fine are you through with the work?"

12

"We just finished the dishes."

"I suppose everybody is listening again tonight."

"I suppose."

"Don't they know I love you? You'd think that was enough for them."

"Maybe it isn't."

"Macia why don't you play a piece on the piano?"

"All right Bill. Which one?"

"Whatever one you like I like them all."

"All right Bill. Wait till I fix the receiver."

And then way out on Cole Creek way west on the other side of the mountains from Denver music tinkling over telephone wires that were brand new and wonderful. His mother before she was his mother before she thought particularly of becoming his mother would go over to the piano the only one on Cole Creek and play the Beautiful Blue Ohio or perhaps My Pretty Red Wing. She would play it clear through and his father in Shale City would be listening and thinking isn't it wonderful I can sit here eight miles away and hold a little piece of black business to my ear and hear far off the music of Macia my beautiful my Macia.

"Could you hear it Bill?"

"Yes. It was lovely."

Then somebody else maybe six miles up or down the line would break into the conversation without being ashamed at all.

"Macia I just picked up the hook and heard you playing. Why don't you play After the Ball is Over? Clem'd like to hear it if you don't mind."

His mother would go back to the piano and play After the Ball is Over and Clem somewhere would be listening to music for maybe the first time in

three or four months. Farmers' wives would be
sitting with their work done and receivers to their
ears listening too and getting dreamy and thinking
about things their husbands wouldn't suspect. And
so it went with everybody up and down the lonesome bed of Cole Creek asking his mother to play
a favorite piece and his father listening from Shale
City and liking it but perhaps growing a little impatient occasionally and saying to himself I wish the
people out on Cole Creek would understand that
this is a courtship not a concert.

Sounds sounds sounds everywhere with the bell
fading out and returning and him so sick and deaf
he wanted to die. He was wallowing in blackness
and far away the telephone bell was ringing with
nobody there to answer it. A piano was tinkling far
far away and he knew his mother was playing it for
his dead father before his father was dead and before she had any thought of him her son. The piano
kept time with the bell and the bell with the piano
and in back of it there was thick silence and a yearning to listen and lonesomeness.

Now the moon shines tonight on pretty Red Wing
The birds are sighing, the night wind crying . . .

ii

His mother was singing in the kitchen. He could hear her singing there and the sound of her voice was the sound of home. She sang the same tune over and over again. She never sang the words to it just the tune in a kind of absent voice as if she were thinking of something else and the singing were only a way of killing time. When she was busiest she always sang.

It was the fall of the year. The poplars and cottonwoods had turned red and yellow. His mother was working and singing in the kitchen over the old coal-burning stove. She was stirring apple butter in a big crock. Or she was canning peaches. The peaches sent a rich spicy smell through the whole house. She was making jelly. The pulp from the fruit hung in a flour sack over the cooler part of the stove. Through the cloth the juices oozed stickily down into a pan. The pan had a thick pinkish-cream scum around its edges. In the center the juice was clear and red.

She was baking bread. She baked bread twice a week. She kept a jar of starter in the ice box from baking time to baking time so she never had to worry about yeast. The bread was heavy and brown and sometimes it swelled two or three inches over the top of the pan. When she took it out of the oven she smeared the brown crust with butter and let it cool. But even better than the bread were the rolls. She baked them to come out of the oven just before supper. They were steaming hot and you put butter inside them and it melted and then you put jam on them or apricot preserves with nuts in the syrup. That was all you wanted for supper although you had to eat other things of course. On summer afternoons you took a thick slice of the bread and put cold butter on it. Then you sprinkled sugar over the butter and that was better than cake. Or you got a thick slice of sweet bermuda onion and put it between two slabs of bread and butter and nobody anywhere in the world had anything more delicious to eat.

In the fall his mother worked from day to day and from week to week scarcely ever getting out of the kitchen. She canned peaches and cherries and raspberries and black berries and plums and apricots and made jams and jellies and preserves and chili sauces. And while she worked she sang. She sang the same hymn in an absent voice without words as if she were thinking of something else all the while.

There was a hamburger man down on Fifth and Main. He was slight and stooped and pasty-faced and always glad to talk with anyone who stopped by his stand. He was the only hamburger man in Shale City so he had a monopoly on the business. People said he was a dope fiend and that sometime he would get dangerous. But he never did and he made the best hamburgers anyone ever ate. He had a gas flare over his gas plate and you could smell the wonderful odor of onions frying there for a block on either side of his stand. He came out about five or six in the afternoons and made hamburgers until ten or eleven. You had to wait if you wanted a sandwich.

His mother loved the hamburger man's sandwiches. On Saturday nights his father worked late at the store. He would go down town on Saturday nights and wait until his father got his pay check. At about a quarter to ten when the store was getting ready to close his father would give him thirty cents for three hamburgers. He would rush with his money over to the hamburger man to get a place in line. He would order three hamburgers to go with lots of onions and sweet mustard. By the time the order was filled his father would already be on the way home. The hamburger man would put the sandwiches in a bag and he would put the bag inside his shirt next to his body. Then he would run all the way home so that the hamburgers would still be warm. He would run through the sharp autumn nights feeling the heat of the hamburgers next to his stomach. Each Saturday night he tried to beat last Saturday's time so the sandwiches would be even warmer. He would get home and pull them out of his shirt front and his mother would eat one right away. By that time his father would be home too. It was a great Saturday night feast. The girls would be in bed being so young and it seemed to him that he had his father and mother completely to himself. He was in a way grown up. He envied the hamburger man because the hamburger man could have all the sandwiches he wanted.

In the fall the snow came. Usually there was snow for Thanksgiving but sometimes it didn't come until middle December. The first snowfall was the most wonderful thing on earth. His father always waked him early his voice booming out about the snow. It was usually a wet snow and it clung to everything it touched. Even the wire fence around the chicken coop in the backyard would hold the snow maybe a half inch deep. The chickens never stopped being puzzled and alarmed about the first snow. They would walk carefully in it and shake their feet and the roosters would talk about it complainingly all day long. The outbuildings were always beautiful and a fence post would have a cap four inches high. The birds in vacant lots would make little patterns in the snow crossed up once in a while by a rabbit track. His father never failed to wake him early when the snow fell. First he rushed to the window to look. Then he got into his heavy clothes and his mackinaw and his boots and his sheepskin gloves and took his flexible flyer and went out with the rest of the kids and didn't come back till his feet were numb and his nose was frosty. The snow was a wonderful thing.

In the spring there were primroses all over the vacant lots. They opened in the morning and closed when the sun grew hot and then opened again in the evening. Each evening the kids went on primrose hunts. They brought back great bouquets of white flowers as big as your hand and put them in flat bowls of water. On May Day they made baskets and filled them with primroses hiding a little candy beneath the flowers. When it was dark they went from house to house and left a basket and knocked on the door and ran away fast into the night.

Lincoln Beechy came to town. It was the first airplane Shale City ever saw. They had it in a tent in the middle of the race track over in the fair grounds. Day in and day out people filed through the tent looking at it. It seemed to be all wire and cloth. People couldn't understand how a man would risk his life just on the strength of a wire. One little wire gone wrong and it meant the end of Lincoln Beechy. Away up in front of the plane ahead of the propellers was a little seat with a stick in front of it. That was where the great aviator sat.

Everyone in Shale City was pleased with the idea of Lincoln Beechy coming to town. It was a wonderful thing. Shale City was really becoming a metropolis. Lincoln Beechy didn't stop at every little stick-in-the-mud town. He stopped only in places like Denver and Shale City and Salt Lake and he was going on to San Francisco. The whole town turned out the day Lincoln Beechy looped the loop. He did it five times. It was the damnedest thing anybody ever saw.

Mr. Hargraves who was superintendent of schools made a speech before the flight. He told about how the invention of the airplane was the greatest step forward man had made in a hundred years. The airplane said Mr. Hargraves would cut down the distance between nations and peoples. The airplane would be a great instrument in making people understand one another in making people love one another. The airplane said Mr. Hargraves was ushering in a new era of peace and prosperity and mutual understanding. Everyone would be friends said Mr. Hargraves when the airplane knitted the world together so that the people of the world understood each other.

After the speech Lincoln Beechy looped the loop five times and left town. A couple months later his airplane fell into San Francisco Bay and Lincoln Beechy was drowned. Shale City felt as if it had lost a resident. The Shale City Monitor ran an editorial. It said that even though the great Lincoln Beechy was dead the airplane the instrument of peace the knitter together of peoples would go on.

His birthday fell in December. Each birthday his mother cooked a big dinner and he had his friends over to the house. Each of his friends also had birthday dinners so there were at least six big affairs during the year for the guys to get together. They usually had chicken and there was always a birthday cake and ice cream. The guys all brought presents. He would never forget the time Glen Hogan brought him a pair of brown silk socks. That was before he had long trousers. The socks seemed to mean a step forward into a grownup future. They were very handsome. After the party he put them on and stared at them for a long while. He got the long pants to go with them three months later.

The guys all liked his father probably because his father liked the guys. After the dinner was over his father always took them all to a show. They would put on their mackinaws and go outside into

the snow and tramp down to the Elysium theatre.
It was great feeling warm on the inside from food
and your face cold on the outside from zero air and
a show to look forward to. He could hear their
footsteps squeaking in the snow even now. He could
see his father leading the pack down to the Elysium.
He remembered that the shows were always good.

In the fall there was the County Fair. There were
bucking bronchos and steers to be bulldogged and
bareback Indian races and trotting races. There was
always a bunch of Indians headed by the great
squaw Chipeta. A street in Shale City was named
after her. The town of Ouray Colorado had been
named after Chief Ouray her husband. The Indians
Chipeta brought with her didn't do much but squat
around and stare but Chipeta herself was full of
smiles and talk about the early days.

A carnival came to town during the fair and you
could see women cut in half and motorcycle riders
defying death inside a straight up and down circular
wall. In the main auditorium of the fair grounds
there were canned fruits gleaming through Mason
jars and displays of embroidery and rows of cakes
and piles of bread and huge squashes and extra-
fancy potatoes. In the livestock pens there were
steers that looked as square as an outhouse and pigs
almost as big as cows and thoroughbred chickens.
Fair week was the biggest week of the year. In a
way it was even bigger than Christmas. You bought
whips with tassels on the ends and it was a mark
of favor if you flicked the legs of a girl you liked.
There was a smell about the fair grounds you never
forgot. A smell you never ceased dreaming of. He

Dalton Trumbo

would always smell it somewhere back in his mind as long as he lived.

In the summer they went out to the big ditch north of town and stripped off their clothes and lay around on its banks and talked. The water would be warm from the summer air and heat would be rising off the brown-gray land like steam. They would swim for a little while then they would go back on the bank and sit around all naked and tan and talk. They would talk about bicycles and girls and dogs and guns. They would talk about camping trips and rabbit hunting and girls and fishing. They would talk about the hunting knives they all wanted but only Glen Hogan had. They would talk about girls.

When they came of an age to take girls out on dates they always took them to the pavilion in the fair grounds. They began to get very dressy. They talked about ties with matching handkerchiefs and they wore brogue shoes and shirts that had bright red and green and yellow stripes in them. Glen Hogan had seven silk shirts. He had most of the girls too. It got to be an important matter whether or not you had a car and it was a very humiliating thing to walk your girl to the pavilion.

Sometimes you didn't have enough money to go to the dance so you would drive lazily by the fair grounds and hear the music coming through the night from the pavilion. The songs all had meaning and the words were very serious. You felt all swelled up inside and you wished you were over there at the pavilion. You wondered who your girl was dancing with. Then you would light a cigarette and talk about something else. It was quite a thing to light a cigarette. You only did it at night when nobody would see you. You made a serious business of holding the cigarette in a properly careless fashion. And the first guy in the bunch able to inhale was the greatest guy on earth until the rest caught up with him.

Down at Jim O'Connell's cigar store the old men sat around and talked about the war. O'Connell's was very cool in the back room. Before Colorado went dry it was a saloon and it still had the smell of beer in the floorboards on damp days. The old men sat there on high chairs and watched the pool tables and spat into big brass spittoons and talked about England and France and in the end about Rooshia. Rooshia was always on the point of starting a big offensive that would push the goddam Germans right back on Berlin. That would be the end of your war.

Then his father decided to leave Shale City. They went to Los Angeles. There he became conscious for the first time about the war. He waked to the war when Roumania entered. It seemed very important. He had never heard of Roumania except in geography classes. But the entry of Roumania into the war occurred on the same day the Los Angeles newspapers carried a story of two young Canadian soldiers who had been crucified by the Germans in full view of their comrades across Nomansland. That made the Germans nothing better than animals and naturally you got interested and wanted Germany to get the tar kicked out of her. Everybody talked about the oil wells and the wheat fields of Roumania and how they would supply the Allies and how this surely was the end of the war. But the Germans walked right through Roumania and they took Bucharest and Queen Marie had to leave her palace. Then his father died and America entered the war and he had to come too and here he was.

He lay and thought oh Joe Joe this is no place for you. This was no war for you. This thing wasn't any of your business. What do you care about making the world safe for democracy? All you wanted to do Joe was to live. You were born and raised in the good healthy country of Colorado and you had no more to do with Germany or England or France or even with Washington D.C. than you had to do with the man in the moon. Yet here you are and it was none of your affair. Here you are Joe and you're hurt worse than you think. You're hurt bad. Maybe it would be a lot better if you were dead and buried on the hill across the river from Shale City. Maybe there are more things wrong with you than you suspect Joe. Oh why the hell did you ever get into this mess anyhow? Because it wasn't your fight Joe. You never really knew what the fight was all about.

He shot up through cool waters wondering whether he'd ever make the surface or not. That was a lot of guff about people sinking three times and then drowning. He'd been rising and sinking for days weeks months who could tell? But he hadn't drowned. As he came to the surface each time he fainted into reality and as he went down again he fainted into nothingness. Long slow faints all of them while he struggled for air and life. He was fighting too hard and he knew it. A man can't fight always. If he's drowning or suffocating he's got to be smart and hold back some of his strength for the last the final the death struggle.

He lay back quietly because he was no fool. If you lie back you can float. He used to float a lot when he was a kid. He knew how to do it. His last strength going into that fight when all he had to do was float. What a fool.

They were working on him. It took him a little

25

while to understand this because he couldn't hear them. Then he remembered that he was deaf. It was funny to lie there and have people in the room who were touching you watching you doctoring you and yet not within hearing distance. The bandages were still all over his head so he couldn't see them either. He only knew that way out there in the darkness beyond the reach of his ears people were working over him and trying to help him.

They were taking part of his bandages off. He could feel the coolness the sudden drying of sweat on his left side. They were working on his arm. He felt the pinch of a sharp little instrument grabbing something and getting a bit of his skin with each grab. He didn't jump. He simply lay there because he had to save his strength. He tried to figure out why they were pinching him. After each pinch there was a little pull in the flesh of his upper arm and an unpleasant point of heat like friction. The pulling kept on in short little jerks with his skin getting hot each time. It hurt. He wished they'd stop. It itched. He wished they'd scratch him.

He froze all over stiff and rigid like a dead cat. There was something wrong about this pricking and pulling and friction heat. He could feel the things they were doing to his arm and yet he couldn't rightly feel his arm at all. It was like he felt inside his arm. It was like he felt through the end of his arm. The nearest thing he could think of to the end of his arm was the heel of his hand. But the heel of his hand the end of his arm was high high high as his shoulder.

Oh Jesus Christ they'd cut his left arm off.

They'd cut it right off at the shoulder he could feel it plain now.

Oh my god why did they do a thing like that to him?

They couldn't do it the dirty bastards they couldn't do it. They had to have a paper signed or something. It was the law. You can't just go out and cut a man's arm off without asking him without getting permission because a man's arm is his own and he needs it. Oh Jesus I have to work with that arm why did you cut it off? Why did you cut my arm off answer me why did you cut my arm off? Why did you why did you why did you?

He went down into the water again and fought and fought and then came up with his belly jumping and his throat aching. And all the time that he was under the water fighting with only one arm to get back he was having conversation with himself about how this thing couldn't possibly happen to him only it had.

So they cut my arm off. How am I going to work now? They don't think of that. They don't think of anything but doing it their own way. Just another guy with a hole in his arm let's cut it off what do you say boys? Sure cut the guy's arm off. It takes a lot of work and a lot of money to fix up a guy's arm. This is a war and war is hell and what the hell and so to hell with it. Come on boys watch this. Pretty slick hey? He's down in bed and can't say anything and it's his tough luck and we're tired and this is a stinking war anyhow so let's cut the damn thing off and be done with it.

My arm. My arm they've cut my arm off. See that

27

stump there? That used to be my arm. Oh sure I had an arm I was born with one I was normal just like you and I could hear and I had a left arm like anybody. But what do you think of those lazy bastards cutting it off?

How's that?

I can't hear either. I can't hear. Write it down. Put it on a piece of paper. I can read all right. But I can't hear. Put it down on a piece of paper and hand the paper to my right arm because I have no left arm.

My left arm. I wonder what they've done with it. When you cut a man's arm off you have to do something with it. You can't just leave it lying around. Do you send it to hospitals so guys can pick it to pieces and see how an arm works? Do you wrap it up in an old newspaper and throw it onto the junk heap? Do you bury it? After all it's part of a man a very important part of a man and it should be treated respectfully. Do you take it out and bury it and say a little prayer? You should because it's human flesh and it died young and it deserves a good sendoff.

My ring.

There was a ring on my hand. What have you done with it? Kareen gave it to me and I want it back. I can wear it on the other hand. I've got to have it because it means something it's important. If you've stolen it I'll turn you in as soon as I get these bandages off you thieving bastards you. If you've stolen it you're grave robbers because my arm that is gone is dead and you've taken the ring from it and you've robbed the dead that's what you've done. Where is my ring Kareen's ring before I go under again? I want the ring. You've got the arm isn't that enough where's my ring Kareen's ring our ring please where is it? The hand it was on is dead and it wasn't meant to be on rotten flesh. It was meant always to be on my living finger on my living hand because it meant life.

"My mother gave it to me. It's a real moonstone. You can wear it."

"It won't fit."

"The little finger silly try the little finger."

"Oh."

"See I said it would fit."

"Little mick."

"Oh Joe I'm so scared kiss me again."

"We shouldn't've turned the lights out. Your old man'll be sore."

"Kiss me. Mike won't care he understands."

"Little mick little mick little mick."

"Don't go please don't go Joe."

"When you're drafted you got to go."

"They'll kill you."

"Maybe. I don't think so."

"Lots of people get killed who don't think so don't go Joe."

"Lots of people come back."

"I love you Joe."

"Little mick."

"I'm not mick I'm bohunk."

"You're half and half but you look mick. You've got eyes and hair like a little mick."

"Oh Joe."

"Don't cry Kareen please don't cry."

29

Suddenly a shadow fell across them and they both looked up.

"Stop that stop it goddam you."

Old Mike Birkman how did he get into the house so quietly was standing above them in the darkness glaring down.

They both lay there on the sofa and stared up at him. He looked like an overgrown dwarf because his back was crooked from twenty-eight years in the coal mines of Wyoming. Twenty-eight years in the mine with an I.W.W. red card and damning everybody. He stood and glared down at them and they made no move.

"I'll have none of this business going on in my house. You think this is the back seat of a flivver? Now get up like a couple decent people. Go on. Get up from there K'reen."

Kareen got up. She was only five feet one. Mike swore it was because she didn't have enough food when she was a kid but that probably wasn't the truth because her mother had been small and Kareen was perfectly formed and healthy and beautiful so beautiful. Mike was liable to exaggerate when he got excited. Kareen looked up at old Mike unafraid.

"He's going away in the morning."

"I know. I know girl. Get into the bedroom. Both of you. Maybe you never get another chance. Go on K'reen."

Kareen took one long look at him and then with her head bent as if she were a very busy child thinking about something walked into the bedroom.

"Go on in there boy. She's scared. Go in and put your arm around her."

He started to go and then he felt Mike's grip

against his shoulder. Mike was looking straight into his face and even in the dark his eyes could be seen.

"You know how to treat her don't you. She's no whore. You know don't you?"

"Yes."

"Go to bed boy."

He turned and went into the bedroom.

An electric candle was burning on one side of the bureau. In the corner of the room beyond the candle Kareen was standing. Her waist was off lying on a chair beside her. She was wearing a slip. As he came in she was twisted around and down a little toward her hip where her hands were trying to undo the fastening of her skirt. She looked up and saw him and just looked without moving her hands or anything. She looked at him like she was seeing him for the first time and didn't know whether to like him or not. She looked at him in a way that made him want to cry.

He walked over and put his arms around her carefully. She leaned to him with her forehead against his chest. Then she turned away and went over to the bed. She pulled the covers down and climbed in clothes and all. She kept her eyes on him all the time as if she was afraid he might say a sharp word or laugh or go away. She made quiet movements under the covers and then her clothes began to drop over the side of the bed from between the covers. When they were all on the floor beside the bed she smiled at him.

He started slowly to take off his shirt not moving his eyes from her. She looked around the room and frowned.

"Joe turn your back."

"Why?"

"I want to get out of bed."

"Why?"

"There's something I forgot. Turn your back."

"No."

"Please."

"No. I'll get it for you."

"I want to get it myself. Turn your back."

"No. I want to see you."

"You can't Joe get my robe."

"All right. I'll do that."

"In the closet. It's red."

He went to the closet and got her robe. It was a thin little thing with flowers printed on it and not enough to cover anybody really. He took it over to the bed holding it a little distance from her.

"Bring it closer."

"Reach for it."

She laughed and then reached out quick and snatched it from him back under the covers. She had to reach so far that he saw the curve of her breast. She laughed softly all the while she struggled under the covers putting the robe on and pulling it down as if she had played a great joke on him. Then she threw the covers back and jumped out of bed and ran in her bare feet into the living room. He saw the bottoms of her feet as they whisked to the floor. They had two arches one through the instep and another that crossed it rising delicately in the ball of her foot and fading away toward the heel. He thought how beautiful her feet are how strong and beautiful they are.

She came back with a bowl filled with red geraniums. She took them over to a little table that stood in front of the window.

She opened the window and then turned slowly around to face him. She was leaning against the little table and kind of hanging onto it with her hands at the same time.

"If you really want to see me"

"But if you don't want me to I don't want to."

She walked over to the closet and turned her back and slipped off the robe. Then she turned around watching her feet all the time and went over to the bed and slipped in between the covers.

He turned out the light and took off his clothes and got into bed beside her. He threw his arm around her a little carelessly as if it were all an accident. She lay very quietly. He moved his leg. A little puff of air came up from between the covers and he could smell her. Clean clean flesh and the smell of soap and sheets. He put his leg next to hers. She whirled to him and threw both of her arms around his neck and held him tight.

"Oh Joe Joe I don't want you to go."

"You think I want to go?"

"I'm afraid."

"Of me?"

"Oh no."

"Little mick."

"It's nice like this isn't it?"

"Ummm."

"Were you ever like this with anyone before?"

"Not with anyone I loved."

"I'm glad."

"It's the truth. You?"

"You shouldn't ask that."

"Why?"

"Because I'm a lady."

"You're a little mick."

"I never was."

"I know."

"But you couldn't've known really oh Joe I wish you'd run away and not go."

"There. My left arm under you. Like a cushion."

"Kiss me."

"Sweet little mick."

"Darling. Oh darling. Oh. Oh my dear my dear my dear my "

They didn't sleep very much. Sometimes they dozed off and awakened and found that they were apart and came back to each other and held one another tight very tight as if they had been lost forever and had just found each other all over again. And all night long Mike was stirring through the house and coughing and mumbling.

When morning came he stood over their bed holding a breadboard which had two breakfasts on it.

"Here you kids eat."

Tough old Mike standing there gentle and grizzled and fierce with bloodshot painful eyes. Mike had been in jail too many times not to be good. Old Mike who hated everybody. He hated Wilson and he hated Hughes and he hated Roosevelt and he hated the socialists because they had only big talk and milk in their veins for blood. He even hated Debs a little although not much. Twenty-eight years in the coal mine had fixed him up for a fine hater. "And now I'm a railroad bull goddam me a railroad bull how's that for a filthy way to make a living?"

34

Mike with his crooked back from the mines standing there with their breakfasts.

"Here you kids. Hurry up and eat. You ain't got much time."

They ate. Mike went grumbling off and didn't come into the room again. When they had eaten they lay for a little while looking up at the ceiling and digesting their food.

"You rumbled."

"I did not. Besides it isn't nice for you to mention it. It was you anyhow."

"It was a cute little rumble. I liked it."

"You're terrible. You get up first."

"No you get up first."

"Oh Joe kiss me don't go."

"Hurry up you damned kids."

"You get up."

"You."

"I'll count—one two three."

They jumped out of bed. It was chilly. They shivered and laughed at each other and almost never got dressed for wanting to stop and kiss.

"Hurry up you damned kids. You'll miss the train and then Joe will be shot by Americans instead of Germans. That would be a goddam shame."

There were four train loads of them leaving that morning and there was a terrible crowd at the station. The whole place the station and the cars and even the locomotives were draped with bunting and the children and women mostly carried flags little flags that they waved vaguely vacantly. There were three bands all seeming to play at once and lots of officers herding people around and songs and the

35

mayor giving an address and people crying and losing each other and laughing and drunk.

His mother and his sisters were there and Kareen was there and Mike was there muttering goddam fools and glaring at everybody and watching Kareen sharply.

"And their lives if necessary that democracy may not perish from the face of the earth"

It's a long way to Tiperrary it's a long way to go

"Don't get scared Kareen. It's all right."

"As that great patriot Patrick Henry said"

Johnny get your gun get your gun get your gun

"As that great patriot George Washington said"

"Goodbye mother goodbye Catherine goodbye Elizabeth. I'll send back half my pay and dad's insurance will hold out till I get back."

And we won't be back till it's over over there

"Step lively boy you're in the army now."

Pack up your troubles in your old kit bag and smile smile smile

"As that great patriot Abraham Lincoln said"

"Where's my boy where's my boy? He's under age can't you see? He just came up from Tucson bout a week ago. They had him in jail for a tramp and I came all the way here to get him back. They let him out of jail if he'd join the army. He's only sixteen except he's big and strong for his age he always was. He's too young I tell you he's just a baby. Where is he my little boy?"

Goodbye maw goodbye paw goodbye mule with your old hee-haw

"As that great patriot Theodore Roosevelt has said"

America I love you you're like a sweetheart to me

"Don't go Joe run away they'll kill you I know it I'll never see you again."

Oh Kareen why do they have a war right now just when we find each other? Kareen we've got more important things than war. Us Kareen you and me in a house. I'll come home at night to you in my house your house our house. We'll have fat happy kids smart kids too. That's more important than a war. Oh Kareen Kareen I look at you and you're only nineteen and you're old like an old woman. Kareen I look at you and I cry inside and I bleed.

Just a baby's prayer at twilight when lights are low

"As that great patriot Woodrow Wilson has said "

There's a silver lining through the dark cloud shining

"All aboard. All aboard."

Over there over there over there over there over there

"Goodbye son. Write us. We'll make out."

"Goodbye mother goodbye Catherine goodbye Elizabeth don't cry."

"For you are Los Angeles' own. May God bless you. May God give us victory."

"All aboard. All aboard."

The yanks are coming the yanks are coming

"Let us pray. Our Father which art in Heaven"

I can't pray. Kareen can't pray. Kareen Kareen this is no time to pray.

"Thy will be done on earth as it is in heaven"

Kareen Kareen I don't want to go. I want to stay here and be with you and work and make money and have kids and love you. But I've got to go.

"For thine is the kingdom and the power and the glory forever and ever Amen."

"Goodbye Mike goodbye Kareen I love you Kareen."

Oh say can you see

"Goodbye mother goodbye Catherine goodbye Elizabeth."

What so proudly we hailed

"You in my arms Kareen forever."

Whose broad stripes and bright stars

Goodbye everybody goodbye. Goodbye my son father brother lover husband goodbye. Goodbye goodbye my mother father brother sister sweetheart wife goodbye and goodbye.

O'er the land of the free and the home of the brave.

"Goodbye Joe."

"Goodbye Kareen."

"Joe dear darling Joe hold me closer. Drop your bag and put both of your arms around me and hold me tightly. Put both of your arms around me. Both of them."

You in both of my arms Kareen goodbye. Both of my arms. Kareen in my arms. Both of them. Arms arms arms arms. I'm fainting in and out all the time Kareen and I'm not catching on quick. You are in my arms Kareen. You in both of my arms. Both of my arms. Both of them. Both

I haven't got any arms Kareen.

My arms are gone.

Both of my arms are gone Kareen both of them. They're gone.

Kareen Kareen Kareen.

They've cut my arms off both of my arms.

Oh Jesus mother god Kareen they've cut off both of them.

Oh Jesus mother god Kareen Kareen Kareen my arms.

iv

It was hot. So hot that he seemed to be burning up inside and out. It was so hot he couldn't breathe. He could only gasp. Far off against the sky there was a foggy line of mountains and moving straight across the desert was the railroad track dancing and leaping in the heat. It seemed that he and Howie were working on the railroad. That was funny. Oh hell things were getting mixed up again. He'd seen all this before. It was like going into a new drug store for the first time and sitting down and suddenly feeling that you've been there many times before and that you've already heard what the clerk is going to say as soon as he comes up to serve you. He and Howie working on the railroad in the heat? Sure. Sure. It was all right. Things were under control.

He and Howie were working there in the hot sun laying that railroad straight through the Uintah desert. And he was so hot he felt he was going to die. He felt that if he could only stop for a little rest he

40

would cool off. But that was the awful thing about a section gang job. You couldn't ever stop. The fellows didn't laugh and kid as you'd think guys would either. They didn't say a word. They just worked.

Looking at a section gang it always seems as if they are working slow. But you have to work slow because you never stop and you have just so much strength. You don't stop because you're afraid. It isn't that you're afraid of the foreman because the foreman never bothers anybody. It's just that you're afraid for the job and of how much the other guy will do. So he and Howie worked slow and steady trying to keep up with the Mexicans.

His head throbbed and he could hear his heart pounding against his ribs and even down in the calves of his legs he could feel the strong pulse beat and yet he couldn't stop work even for a minute. His breath came shorter and shorter and it seemed that his lungs were too small to hold the air he had to get into them if he was going to keep alive. It was a hundred and twenty-five in the shade and there wasn't any shade and he felt like he was smothering under a white hot blanket and all he could think was I've got to stop I've got to stop I've got to stop.

They stopped for lunch.

It was their first day on the gang and he and Howie naturally thought they would be supplied with lunch from the hand car. But they weren't. When the foreman saw they had nothing to eat he said something to a couple of the Mexicans. The Mexicans came over and offered them something out of their lunch pails. The Mexicans were eating fried egg sandwiches all crusted over with red pepper.

He and Howie just grunted no thanks and flopped on their backs. Then they turned over on their stomachs because the sun was so hot it would have burned out their eye balls even with the lids closed. The Mexicans just sat and chewed on their fried egg sandwiches and stared at them.

All of a sudden there was the noise of the Mexicans getting up so he and Howie rolled over to see what was happening. The whole gang was starting down the tracks on a slow gallop. The foreman just sat and watched the gang. They asked the foreman what the idea was and the foreman said the boys were going to take a swim.

The idea of a swim was too much. He and Howie jumped up and ran along after them. The way the foreman spoke they thought they were going just a little piece down the track. But it turned out they ran two miles before they came to a canal maybe ten feet wide and mud-colored and beached on both sides with a solid mass of tumbleweeds. The Mexicans started pulling their clothes off. He and Howie wondered how they figured to make it into the water without getting full of thistles. They decided there must be some path through the weeds or the Mexicans wouldn't have tackled the swim in the first place. By the time they were undressed the Mexicans were splashing around in the ditch and laughing and yelling.

It turned out there wasn't any path through the tumbleweeds after all. They were ashamed to stand there so naked and white compared to the rest and do nothing about it. So they began jumping through the tumbleweeds until they were in the water. The water was hot and it smelled of alkali but that didn't make any difference. It was like an April shower. He thought about the Y.M.C.A. swimming pool in Shale City. He thought my gosh these guys act as if this was the greatest swimming hole in the world. He thought I'll bet they were never in a swimming pool in their lives. He was standing there with the mud of the ditch bottom up above his ankles when the Mexicans began climbing out and putting their clothes on again. The swim was over.

By the time he and Howie got back to their clothes they were whiskered with thistles to the hips. They noticed that the Mexicans didn't even bother to pick the thistles out. Some of the Mexicans were already starting on the trip back to the hand car so they sort of brushed the thistles off their legs and leaped into their clothes. Then they ran the two miles back and lunch was over and it was time to go to work again.

As the afternoon wore on he and Howie began to stumble at their work and finally to fall. The foreman didn't say anything when they fell down and neither did the Mexicans. The Mexicans just stopped and waited for them to get up staring like babies all the while. When they stumbled back to their feet they began tugging at the rails again. Every muscle in their bodies ached and still they had to keep on working. Most of the skin had worn off their hands. Every time they grabbed the hot rail-tongs and lifted they could taste the pain of raw hands clear into their mouths. The thistles in their feet and legs seemed to go deeper and deeper with every step they took and they festered and there was no time to stop and pick them out.

But the aches and bruises and the awful weariness

weren't the worst things. His body could keep up somehow but it was the things inside of him that began to strain and roar. His lungs got so dry that they squeaked with each breath. His heart swelled from pumping so hard. He got a little panic-stricken because he knew he couldn't keep it up and he knew he had to. He wanted to die if that would get him out of work. The ground began to rise and fall beneath him and things took on a strange color and the man standing right beside him seemed miles off floating in a fog. There was nothing real but pain.

The whole afternoon was a mixture of stumbling on his knees in the dust and fighting for breath and feeling his stomach inside him swell and jerk and draw up hard. He tried to think of Diane. He tried to think of what she looked like. He tried to find her there in the desert so he would have something to tie to. But he couldn't bring her face before his eyes. He couldn't even imagine her.

Suddenly he thought oh Diane you're not worth it. You can't be worth it. No one on earth except maybe a guy's mother could be worth so much pain. Yet working there in the midst of pain he tried to figure out excuses for Diane. Maybe she really hadn't meant to cheat on him. Maybe she had dated Glen Hogan because she couldn't find any other way out. If that was true and he hoped it was true then it was awfully silly for him to be away out here in the desert forgetting it all with a bunch of Mexicans when he might just as well be back in the cool shade of Shale City enjoying summer vacation and thinking maybe I'll have a date with Diane tonight.

He thought girls are a terrible thing all right. Girls are probably all untrue and faithless and they try to smash a guy but you've just got to expect it from them. You've had to expect it from them and learn to forgive them because it stood to reason that if you rushed away like he and Howie had and went into the middle of a desert and decided you would bury yourselves there for the whole three months' summer vacation why nobody suffered but you. And that left the girl back there in Shale City to go out with Glen Hogan as much as she wanted to. Tugging and stumbling and trying to breathe he suddenly had an awful feeling come over him. He was asking himself a question. He was saying to himself Joe Bonham have you been a fool?

Somebody hollered out that it was quitting time and things began to dissolve slowly in front of his eyes. When he got them back into focus he was lying on his stomach with his head hanging over the side of the hand car and Howie lying beside him. He remembered looking down at the ground as it ran like water in front of his eyes and hearing those Mexicans singing. They were taking turns pumping away on that hand car to get them back to the bunkhouse. He just lay there gagging a little and listening to them sing.

The bunkhouse had a dirt floor. It was a sort of shed with a tin roof. It was so hot inside that he wanted to reach out with his hands for air to stuff into his lungs. The bunks were wood one on top of the other. He and Howie staggered to a pair of bunks that were together. They didn't even bother to unroll their bedding. They flopped on the bunks and lay there quiet and still. The foreman came up and asked if they wanted him to show them where they

45

could get dinner. But they didn't pay any attention to him. They just lay back and closed their eyes.

He had reached a funny state. It was the first time in his life he had ever felt that way. No one part of his body hurt more than any other part so the pain everywhere stopped and he was only numb and sleepy. He thought about Diane again. Not for very long but she was the last thought in his mind before the darkness. He thought about Diane tiny and cute and scared the first time he kissed her. Oh Diane he thought how could you have done such a thing? How could you have done it? And then somebody was shaking him.

They might have been shaking him for hours for all he knew. He opened his eyes. He was still in the bunkhouse. It was dark and the air was filled with sighs. There was a smell of smoke in the place. The Mexicans had cooked their supper over a fire in the middle of the floor. There was a hole in the tin roof for the smoke to escape through. He could see the stars through it flickering like something in a fever dream. He gagged. The smell of food and smoke in the air. Wasn't it just like a Mexican to want something piping hot for supper after spending a whole day in the bottom of hell?

It was Howie shaking him.

"Wake up. It's ten o'clock."

He didn't know whether it was night or whether his eye sockets had just burned out and he couldn't tell sunlight from dark.

"Morning or night?"

"Night."

"Tonight or last night?"

"Last night I guess. Hey look what I got. They just sent it over from the dispatcher's office."

Howie stuck something in front of his face and turned his pocket flashlight on it. They had remembered to bring a flashlight even if they had forgotten gloves. It was a telegram Howie was showing him. The corners of it were all bloody where Howie had been holding it. It read Dear Howie why were you so impetuous stop I am miserable thinking what you have done stop please forgive me and come right back to Shale City stop I hate Glen Hogan stop love Onie.

Even in the dimness of the bunkhouse he could see the happiness on Howie's face. So Onie hated Glen Hogan did she? Well he knew why and if Howie didn't know why then Howie was a fool. Onie hated Glen Hogan because Glen had thrown her over for Diane. He thought about this for a little bit and about how much prettier Diane was than Onie and about how the whole thing showed what good judgment Glen Hogan had. Then he saw that Howie was waiting for an answer. When he tried to answer he found he could only whisper.

"Why do you have to wake a guy up who needs sleep as bad as I do just to show him that?"

"Because I got it all figured out."

"Uh."

Howie began to whisper very excitedly.

"It's just like this. For fellows like you and me to be out here slaving our best years away on a section gang is just as if girls nice girls like Onie and Diane suddenly decided to become washerwomen."

He didn't say anything. He just lay there and

thought about it. He could see the point all right. The idea of Diane being a washerwoman was so awful he just closed his eyes again. Howie was whispering at him.

"Of course since Onie feels that way I hardly know what to do about the poor kid."

He just lay there with his eyes closed saying nothing.

"It isn't as if I didn't have a reason to go back. It's almost as if it was my duty to."

He just lay there limp. But he was listening to Howie very closely.

"The dispatcher says there's a gravel train going through here tonight bound for Shale City."

Still he didn't say anything. Still he listened.

"It would get us there in an hour."

He kind of moved his leg to show he was still awake listening.

"That gravel train goes through here in ten minutes."

He jumped off his bunk and in one motion had his bed roll over his shoulders. Howie stared at him in surprise.

"What you doing?"

He gave Howie a look to show the whole thing was on Howie's shoulders.

"Well if you're bound and determined to back out on our agreement I guess there's nothing I can do to stop you. If we're going to get that gravel train we better be getting outside."

Most of the way riding into Shale City he thought about Bill Harper. He thought to himself only last night I hit Bill Harper. He thought to himself Bill

48

Harper was my best friend and he was telling me the truth and I hit him for it. He lay back against the gravel and stared up at the stars. He thought how he and Bill Harper had sat in the drug store and how Bill Harper had hemmed and hawed and how he had finally come to the point. He remembered all over again the rage he felt when Bill Harper told him that Diane was going out that night with Glen Hogan. He knew it was probably true or Bill Harper wouldn't have told him. Yet he had stood up and he had called Bill Harper a liar and he had hit Bill Harper and knocked him down and then he had walked out of the drug store alone.

On the way home he had run into Diane and Glen Hogan just getting out of Glen's roadster and going into the Elysium theatre. Then he knew that Bill Harper had been telling him the truth. He knew that Diane had been cheating on him.

Down the block he met Howie. Howie had been having trouble with Onie over Glen Hogan so they both decided to leave it all and go out into the desert and work like men and forget about it. It wasn't like he and Howie were the same. Howie had never been able to keep a girl. He kind of resented Howie including him in his class. But he wanted to get away so badly that when Howie suggested it he said let's go tomorrow.

He lay on the gravel car and remembered all the camping trips and the swell times he and Bill Harper had had together. He remembered the first time either of them took a girl out. They made it a foursome because they were so scared. He remembered the time Major his pup was run over and how Bill came over that night with his old man's car and took him riding

out in the country until after midnight and didn't
say a word all that time because Bill knew how he
felt. He remembered lots of other times too and he
thought Bill Harper is too good a friend to lose over
any girl. He thought Bill is too good a friend to lose
even over Diane and tomorrow I will tell him so.
Tomorrow I will go over to his house and say Bill
let's forget about it. Bill let's be friends because it
won't ever happen again.

And then as the gravel train got closer to Shale
City he thought back to Diane again. In the coolness
of the night he could bring her face up before his
mind. He hadn't been able to do it out there on the
desert. He could bring her face up before his mind
and she was smiling. He thought Howie believed he
had lost Onie but he hadn't because Onie admitted
she was wrong and asked him to come back. He
thought besides I don't want Diane running around
with Glen Hogan. Anybody but Glen Hogan. Just
because Glen had a good looking car he seemed to
think he could take liberties with a girl that the ordinary guy would never think of. He felt scary whenever he thought of Diane and Glen Hogan together.
He saw where it was more or less his duty to see
Diane and talk to her like a brother and tell her
about Glen Hogan. He knew that he had to save
Diane the embarrassment of finding out for herself
what kind of guy Glen Hogan was. He must do that
even at the expense of his pride.

They dropped off the gravel train just outside the
station because they didn't want anybody to see them
they were such sights. They walked for two blocks
and then Howie stopped.

"Well I'll be leaving you here."

"Where are you going?"

"Thought I'd drop by Onie's house."

Howie said it in a dreamy kind of way and a little insinuating too because he knew there was no place for Joe to go but home. Howie who could never keep a girl. Huh!

Howie walked off into the darkness. He was all alone. He started home. Shale City seemed like the prettiest town in the world that night. The sky was pale blue and there were about a million stars shining. The trees were all black-green and a cool breeze was playing through them. It seemed all of a sudden as if the desert and the section gang had never existed at all. He was awfully tired but there was no one watching him to see that he kept moving and he knew he could stop and rest whenever he wanted to and somehow he had got his second wind so he didn't even notice the weight of his bed roll. He just seemed to drift along there in the cool. It was a little after eleven o'clock.

And then he suddenly knew why he felt so good when all the time he should be feeling bad. It was because he was on Diane's street. He hadn't deliberately planned to be there because it was a couple of blocks out of his way and he was really awfully tired. It just seemed that something pulled him over to that street and he was glad for it. Even on ordinary nights he always had the funniest feeling when he got near Diane's house. He always got tight in his throat and half way excited and half way scared whenever he came near to where she lived.

Then all of a sudden he thought here you can't be passing Diane's house all bloody-handed and dirty like you are now. You can't run the risk of letting her see you in this condition. So he went across the street and started walking on his tip toes as if she might be asleep and the very sound of his footsteps might wake her and frighten her. And all the time something inside him was saying tomorrow you'll see her tomorrow you'll see her tomorrow you'll see her.

Then just across from her place he stopped still and quit breathing. Diane was there on the front steps with her arms around somebody and somebody's arms around her. They were kissing. He didn't do anything. He just stood there a little behind a tree and watched. He didn't want to watch and yet he wanted to watch more than anything else he could think of. He felt ashamed watching and yet he couldn't move one inch from the spot. He just stood there. He just stood there and watched.

Pretty soon the guy she was kissing let her go and Diane ran up the steps in that funny little way she always had and turned just as she got to the door to smile. He couldn't see her face of course but he knew she was smiling. A minute of that and then whoever she had been kissing turned away and began coming down the walk. He was whistling. He was whistling softly and kind of bouncing up and down as he walked away from having kissed Diane. When he got out from between the trees the starlight fell on his face. It was Bill Harper.

Still he stood there. Bill Harper walked on down the street and turned the corner. The light in Diane's living room went on and off. Next the light in her bedroom came on. He saw her shadow on the curtain twice as she crossed. Then the light went off.

He stood there and thought goodbye Diane goodbye.

Then he started walking home.

Every muscle in his body was sore. His hands and his stomach and his head throbbed and burned. The bed roll seemed to weigh a hundred pounds almost. But that wasn't what hurt him. It was something inside of him kept saying you're no good. You're just no good.

People would ask why don't I see you and Diane together any more? and there would be nothing he could say. People would ask what's the matter with you and Bill Harper that we don't see you around any more? and there would be nothing he could say. His dad would ask how come you got a job on the section gang and stayed only one day? and there would be nothing he could say.

It was all over. It was something he could never explain. Something nobody would understand. He had lost the only friend he might have told it to. Because he knew that he and Bill could never again be what they had been. They might shake hands and say forget it old man and start bumming around together a little but it wouldn't be the same. And both of them would know it. Both of them would know that Diane was there between them. Both of them would also know that Diane probably didn't care but that wouldn't make things any different for them. They'd never be able to explain it even to themselves.

But more than that he thought about Diane. It seemed like dying to think he would never see her again really and that he would never be close to her again and that they would never laugh and kid each other again. It wasn't Glen Hogan who had done it.

He could have forgiven her for Glen Hogan. He could have forgiven her for that and tried to make it all up. The awful thing was that she had done something he couldn't forgive her for ever no matter how much he wanted to. And he did want to. He did want to awfully. But he never could.

Going to bed he thought oh why does a guy have to go through something like this? He thought why don't they take him out and shoot him while there's still something worth while in him? He thought why everybody has a best friend. Even guys in the penitentiary probably have best friends somewhere. But I haven't. He thought even Howie has a girl. Even those Mexicans singing on their way out of the desert have girls. But I haven't. He thought why everybody can find some little spark of self respect inside himself. Even a murderer or a thief or a dog or an ant has something that keeps its head up and going. But I haven't.

That night in bed was the first time he ever cried over a girl. He just lay there and bawled like a kid. His hands were bloody and his legs were full of thistles and his eyes were full of tears and he was sick at heart. It took him a long time to go to sleep.

It all seemed so real at the time and now it wasn't real at all. That was a long time ago. That was in Shale City. That was before he came to Los Angeles. That was when he was a kid in high school. It seemed so long ago. Somewhere probably in Colorado Glen Hogan and Howie were still kicking around. He had got a letter once saying Bill Harper had been killed at Belleau Wood. Bill Harper was a lucky guy. Bill Harper had got Diane and then he had been killed.

Oh Christ he was all mixed up again. He didn't know where he was or what he was doing. But he was cooling off. He wasn't burning up any more. He was just light headed and confused and he couldn't figure things out. Everything was a mess but at least he was cool.

▼

He couldn't get used to the way things were melting into each other. Sometimes he was drifting on top of white clouds frightened at his smallness in the midst of a thing so big as the sky. Sometimes he was cushioned in soft pillows that had a way of sliding him feet first over rough and uneven ground. But mostly he was floating in some backwash of the Colorado River where it wandered through Shale City. He was lying in the water of a river that ran through home long before he came to Los Angeles long before he met Kareen long long before he went away on a bunting-covered train with the mayor making speeches.

He was floating on his back. There were willows near the edge of the water and sweet clover. There was hot sunshine on his face but his stomach and back were cool from water that had been snow in the mountains not long ago. He was floating there and thinking about Kareen.

It's fine Kareen floating here. Lie back more like
this like that. Isn't it nice Kareen I love it I love
you. Float Kareen keep your head out of the water
so you can breathe. Keep real close to me Kareen
isn't it swell floating here not going anywhere and
not even caring to go anywhere? Just letting the
river take care of things. Nothing to do and nowhere
to go. Being on top of the river cool and hot and
thoughtful yet not thinking a thing.

Stay closer Kareen. Don't go away. Closer closer
Kareen and watch out for the water coming over
your face. I can't turn over on my stomach to swim
Kareen I can only float so please don't go so far
away. Kareen where are you I can't find you and the
water was coming over your face. Don't sink Kareen
don't let the water come over your face. Come back
Kareen you'll choke you'll fill up like I'm filling up.
You'll go down Kareen watch out please watch out.
Come back Kareen. You're gone. You weren't even
there. Just me alone in the river with water coming
over my nose and mouth and eyes.

The water was washing over his face and he
couldn't stop it. It was like his head was too heavy
for his body and he couldn't let it lie back without
sinking. Or maybe his body was too light for his
head so that there wasn't enough weight to balance
his head and keep it high. The water was lapping
over his eyes and nose and mouth and he was sput-
tering from it. It seemed like he was going feet first
on his back against the stream only he was going like
a sled with his feet and legs entirely out of the water
and his head below the surface. He was going faster
and faster and if he didn't stop why he'd drown from
so much water rushing over his face.

He was beginning to drown already. He strained the muscles of his neck trying to raise his nose out of the water but it wouldn't come up. He tried to swim but how can a man swim if he hasn't got any arms? He sank down and down and down and finally he drowned. It seemed like he drowned without even a struggle way down in the dark bottom of the river while above him maybe only six or eight feet there was sunlight and willows and sweet clover and air. He drowned without a struggle because he couldn't struggle. He didn't seem to have anything to struggle with. It was like a bad dream where someone is chasing you and you're scared to death only there's nothing to do about it because you can't run. Your legs are stuck in concrete and you can't move a muscle. That was why he drowned.

He lay there under the water and thought what a shame it is to drown when you're maybe only six or eight feet from air and sunlight. What a goddam shame it is to drown when if you could only stand up and stretch your hand above your head you might touch a willow branch trailing in the water like the hair of a girl like Kareen's hair. But when you're drowned you can't stand up. When you're dead and drowned there's nothing left except time going on and on like water over your body.

Things began to shoot back and forth in front of his eyes. Rockets and bombs and pinwheels and curves of fire and great white flares whirled through his head and sank into the soft wet part of his brain with a hissing sound. He could hear the hissing very plainly. It was like the escape of steam from a locomotive. He could hear explosions and howls and whines and words that didn't mean anything and whistles too high and shrill that they cut through his ears like knives. Everything was dazzling and deafening. It hurt so much that he thought all the pain in the world was trapped somewhere between his forehead and the back of his skull and trying to hammer its way out. The pain was so bad that all he could think of was please please please I'd rather die.

Then things quieted down all of a sudden. Everything went still inside his head. The lights before his eyes snapped out as quickly as if somebody had shut them off with a switch. The pain went away too. The only feeling he had was the strong throb of blood in his brain swelling and contracting his head. But it was peaceful. It was painless. It was such a relief that he came out of his drowning. He could think.

He thought well kid you're deaf as a post but there isn't the pain. You've got no arms but you don't hurt. You'll never burn your hand or cut your finger or smash a nail you lucky stiff. You're alive and you don't hurt and that's much better than being alive and hurting. There are lots of things a deaf guy without arms can do if he doesn't hurt so much he goes crazy from pain. He can get hooks or something for arms and he can learn to read lips and while that doesn't exactly put him on top of the world still he's not drowned in the bottom of a river with pain tearing his brain to pieces. He's still got air and he's not struggling and he's got willow trees and he can think and he's not in pain.

He couldn't understand why the nurses or whoever had charge of him wouldn't lay him out level. The lower half of him was light as a feather while his head and chest were dead weights. That was why he had thought he was drowning. His head was too low.

If he could move whatever was under his legs and bring his body to an even level he'd feel better. He wouldn't have that drowning dream any more.

He started to kick out with his feet to move what was under his legs. He only started because he didn't have any legs to kick with. Somewhere just below his hip joints they had cut both of his legs off.

No legs.

No more running walking crawling if you have no legs. No more working.

No legs you see.

Never again to wiggle your toes. What a hell of a thing what a wonderful beautiful thing to wiggle your toes.

No no.

If he could only think of real things he would destroy this dream of having no legs. Steamships loaves of bread girls Kareen machine guns books chewing gum pieces of wood Kareen but thinking of real things didn't help because it wasn't a dream.

It was the truth.

That was why his head had seemed lower than his legs. Because he had no legs. Naturally they seemed light. Air is light too. Even a toenail is heavy compared to air.

He had no arms and no legs.

He threw back his head and started to yell from fright. But he only started because he had no mouth to yell with. He was so surprised at not yelling when he tried that he began to work his jaws like a man who has found something interesting and wants to test it. He was so sure the idea of no mouth was a dream that he could investigate it calmly. He tried to work his jaws and he had no jaws. He tried to run his tongue around the inside of his teeth and over the roof of his mouth as if he were chasing a raspberry seed. But he didn't have any tongue and he hadn't any teeth. There was no roof to his mouth and there was no mouth. He tried to swallow but he couldn't because he had no palate and there weren't any muscles left to swallow with.

He began to smother and pant. It was as if someone had pushed a mattress over his face and was holding it there. He was breathing hard and fast now but he wasn't really breathing because there wasn't any air passing through his nose. He didn't have a nose. He could feel his chest rise and fall and quiver but not a breath of air was passing through the place where his nose used to be.

He got a wild panicky eagerness to die to kill himself. He tried to calm his breathing to stop breathing entirely so he would suffocate. He could feel the muscles at the bottom of his throat close tight against the air but the breathing in his chest kept right on. There wasn't any air in his throat to be stopped. His lungs were sucking it in somewhere below his throat.

He knew now that he was surely dying but he was curious. He didn't want to die until he had found out everything. If a man has no nose and no mouth and no palate and no tongue why it stands to reason he might be shy a few other parts as well. But that was nonsense because a man in that shape would be dead. You couldn't lose that much of yourself and still keep on living. Yet if you knew you had lost them and were thinking about it why then you must be alive because dead men don't think. Dead men aren't curious and he was sick with curiosity so he must not be dead yet.

He began to reach out with the nerves of his face. He began to strain to feel the nothingness that was there. Where his mouth and nose had been there must now be nothing but a hole covered with bandages. He was trying to find out how far up that hole went. He was trying to feel the edges of the hole. He was grasping with the nerves and pores of his face to follow the borders of that hole and see how far up they extended.

It was like staring into complete darkness with your eyes popping out of your head. It was a process of feeling with his skin of exploring with something that couldn't move where his mind told it to. The nerves and muscles of his face were crawling like snakes toward his forehead.

The hole began at the base of his throat just below where his jaw should be and went upward in a widening circle. He could feel his skin creeping around the rim of the circle. The hole was getting bigger and bigger. It widened out almost to the base of his ears if he had any and then narrowed again. It ended somewhere above the top of what used to be his nose.

The hole went too high to have any eyes in it.

He was blind.

It was funny how calm he was. He was quiet just like a storekeeper taking spring inventory and saying to himself I see I have no eyes better put that down in the order book. He had no legs and no arms and no eyes and no ears and no nose and no mouth and no tongue. What a hell of a dream. It must be a dream. Of course sweet god it's a dream. He'd have to wake up or he'd go nuts. Nobody could live like that. A person in that condition would be dead and he wasn't dead so he wasn't in that condition. Just dreaming.

But it wasn't a dream.

He could want it to be a dream forever and that wouldn't change things. Because he was alive alive. He was nothing but a piece of meat like the chunks of cartilage old Prof Vogel used to have in biology. Chunks of cartilage that didn't have anything except life so they grew on chemicals. But he was one up on the cartilage. He had a mind and it was thinking. That's more than Prof Vogel could ever say of his cartilages. He was thinking and he was just a thing.

Oh no. No no no.

He couldn't live like this because he would go crazy. But he couldn't die because he couldn't kill himself. If he could only breathe he could die. That was funny but it was true. He could hold his breath and kill himself. That was the only way left. Except that he wasn't breathing. His lungs were pumping air but he couldn't stop them from doing it. He couldn't live and he couldn't die.

No no no that can't be right.

No no.

Mother.

Mother where are you?

Hurry mother hurry hurry hurry and wake me up. I'm having a nightmare mother where are you? Hurry mother. I'm down here. Here mother. Here in the darkness. Pick me up. Rockabye baby. Now I lay me down to sleep. Oh mother hurry because I can't wake up. Over here mother. When the wind blows the cradle will rock. Hold me up high high.

Mother you've gone away and forgotten me. Here I am. I can't wake up mother. Wake me up. I can't move. Hold me. I'm scared. Oh mother mother sing to me and rub me and bathe me and comb my hair and wash out my ears and play with my toes and clap my hands together and blow my nose and kiss my eyes and mouth like I've seen you do with Elizabeth like you must have done with me. Then I'll wake up and I'll be with you and I'll never leave or be afraid or dream again.

Oh no.

I can't. I can't stand it. Scream. Move. Shake something. Make a noise any noise. I can't stand it. Oh no no no.

Please I can't. Please no. Somebody come. Help me. I can't lie here forever like this until maybe years from now I die. I can't. Nobody can. It isn't possible.

I can't breathe but I'm breathing. I'm so scared I can't think but I'm thinking. Oh please please no. No no. It isn't me. Help me. It can't be me. Not me. No no no.

Oh please oh oh please. No no no please no. Please.

Not me.

vi

At the bakery he walked all night long. He walked eleven miles every night. He walked with his legs on the cement floor and his arms in the air swinging free. He hardly ever got tired. When you got to thinking about it it wasn't bad. Walking all night long and working hard and getting eighteen dollars at the end of the week for your trouble. Not bad.

Friday nights were always the heaviest in the night shipping department because on Saturday morning the drivers would take out enough bread and pies and cakes and rolls to last their customers over Sunday. That made a hell of a lot of work and a hell of a lot of walking on Friday nights. But it wasn't bad. They always sent to the Midnight Mission for an extra man to work with the crew on Friday nights. The guys from the Mission came stinking of disinfectant and looking very bedraggled and embarrassed. They knew that anyone who smelled the disinfectant knew they were bums on charity.

They didn't like that and how could you blame them?
They were always humble and when they were bright
enough they worked hard. Some of them weren't
bright. Some of them couldn't even read the orders
on the bins. One of them came from the turpentine
country in Georgia. He'd never been to school at
all. Most of the lazy ones came from Texas.

One night a Porto Rican came up from the Mission. His name was Jose. Things were always pretty
scrambled up in the shipping room on Friday nights
with boxes and dollies and racks scattered through
the aisles and guys hollering and the conveyor belts
rattling away and the rotary ovens upstairs screeching as they moved on hot greaseless plates. It was
pretty much of a mess and most of the Mission guys
were confused when they first came to work. But not
Jose. He looked over the place and listened quietly
to instructions and then went to work. He was tall
with brown eyes and he was pretty good looking for
a Mexican or Porto Rican or whatever he was.
There was something about him that told you he was
a little different from the other Mission guys or that
maybe he had been a little luckier than the rest.

On Friday nights all the guys ate their lunches up
in the men's can instead of going out to a restaurant
because there were benches and lockers there and
you could sit down on the benches and eat your
lunch in a hurry and get back to work. Jose hadn't
brought any lunch so the guys stole a pint of milk
from the bakery ice-box and gave him a roll with it.
Jose was very grateful. While he munched his roll
and drank his milk he talked. He said that California
was a wonderful country. He said it was even more
wonderful than his Porto Rico. He said that it was

getting spring now and soon he would be able to sleep in the park. He said California was a great country for people who had no place to sleep because it didn't get so cold and you could wrap up in an overcoat in the park and get a very good night's sleep thank you. He said he wished he could get a steady job at the bakery because then he could manage to keep clean. He didn't like to be dirty and he didn't like the disinfectant they put in the water at the Mission. There were a lot of poor men down at the Mission who didn't seem to mind the disinfectant but he minded it very much.

He said he had come to California to go into the movies. No he didn't want to be an actor. But there should be many jobs for a young man like himself with ambition in a business as great as the movies. He said that he thought he might like to work in the research department at one of the studios. Perhaps someone could give him some information about getting a job in a studio yes?

The guys just looked at him and grunted. If any of them knew how to get work in a studio wouldn't they have done it long ago instead of sticking around this lousy bakery? No. Nobody knew how to get work for Jose in a studio.

Jose just shrugged. It was pretty hard he said. When he came to New York things were going very well for him and then a very rich girl fell in love with him and he had to come away from there.

A rich girl fallen in love with you Jose?

Yes. He had got a job as chauffeur for a very rich family that lived on Fifth Avenue and things were very well and then the daughter of the family took a liking to him so Jose and the daughter struck a bargain. The daughter wanted to learn Spanish and Jose wanted to improve his English so they started trading lessons. And then the girl she fell in love with him and wanted to marry him and so he had to come away from New York and he came to California.

The guys sitting around in the can just looked at each other and didn't say anything. Everybody who came from the Mission had a line. Everybody had been way up in the money and then wham something had happened and now they were in the Mission. Long ago the guys as the bakery learned that it was no use to argue with guys from the Mission. No matter how closely you questioned them and no matter how many of their stories you proved were lies they still stuck to them. They had to stick to them. Their stories were their only excuse for being what they were so in time the guys at the bakery came to accept the stories told by the guys from the Mission and to say nothing. So after Jose got through with his talking they grunted and went back to work again.

Next week was Easter and that meant hot cross buns and that meant there would have to be lots of extra help because the shipping crew couldn't put out twenty or thirty thousand dozen hot cross buns without extra men. So Jody Simmons offered Jose a job for the week and Jose took it. He was such a good worker on hot cross buns that when Larruping Larry quit Jose got Larry's job. He was very grateful and very quiet. He was also pleased that the weather was warmer. He was sleeping in the park and that was a wonderful thing. You saved money and Jose needed money for clothes. A man who is going to work in the studios must be well dressed said Jose.

Then one day Jose came in with a letter. He was very puzzled. He showed it to the guys and asked their advice. Americans were such strange people he said and you never knew what their customs were exactly. So what should a gentleman do under these circumstances?

The guys all read Jose's letter. It was on a very expensive piece of stationery and written in a woman's hand. At the top of the page was a tiny little engraved address on Fifth Avenue in New York. It was a letter from the girl Jose had been telling about. In the letter she said she wished he would give her his address so she wouldn't have to be writing him general delivery all the time. She had come into some money of her own just a little over a half a million dollars and as soon as she found out where Jose was living she was coming to Los Angeles to marry him.

This gave the guys at the bakery something to think about. Jose might be full of bull like all the other Mission bums but it began to look like this girl of his was the real thing. Jesus Christ they said to Jose don't be a damn fool marry the girl. Send her your address and let her come out just as fast as she can and let her bring all her jack with her and marry her before she changes her mind. But Jose shook his head. He said there wasn't any danger of her changing her mind because like he had said the girl was crazy about him. And certainly he had no objections to marrying a girl with money. In fact he thought the only intelligent thing for a young man without money to do was to marry a young lady who had money. But he wanted also to love the girl with money that he would marry some day. This girl it was too bad but he didn't love her.

Well I'm a sonofabitch said the guys at the bakery you can learn to love her can't you? No said Jose sorrowfully I cannot. He just wanted to know what the American custom about such things was and how he could write the girl and explain to her. Was it polite for an American gentleman to tell an American girl he didn't love her? But no of course not that would be ungallant. Would it not be better to have a friend maybe one of the people of the bakery write to the girl and explain to her that Jose had shot himself because of his love and now was cremated? Jose was willing to do anything to make it right.

By this time all the guys figured Jose was crazy. But they also figured he was kind of smart crazy. When he told tall stories about his native Porto Rico the guys paid more attention to him figuring that since his story about the girl was true there might be a fifty-fifty chance that his stories about Porto Rico were also true. Jose was a very funny guy but then the bakery was full of funny guys and it was just as well not to question them too closely. You took them as they came and said nothing.

After about a month of this Jose came in one night with a very worried look on his face.

What's the matter Jose? Why do you look so down in the dumps Jose? Jose sighed and frowned. He had run into a very serious problem he said. What problem Jose? He had been out all day as usual he said looking for a job and he had found the job.

They all got interested then because everybody at the bakery wanted a better job only none of them ever found one. Where did you get this better job Jose? In a studio of course said Jose. That is why I came to California. Didn't I tell you I came to find work in the studios?

Nobody said anything. They just stared at Jose. From anybody else this would have seemed like more bull but from Jose they knew it was the truth. How did you like that? As far as the guys at the bakery were concerned the studios might just as well be in China as in Hollywood. They paid good dough but nobody except an uncle or maybe a nephew could crack them. Yet Jose just as calm as a cucumber had walked into one and got what he wanted.

How did you get this job Jose? I asked for it said Jose. Oh said the guys at the bakery. Then they sat around and stared at him some more. Finally somebody spoke up and said Jose what's all this about a problem and why are you so worried?

Jose looked surprised. Anybody should know that he said. He had come to California and he had been without money and he had been full of disinfectant from the Midnight Mission and he had been very unhappy. Then this nice gentleman Jody Simmons had accepted him into the bakery and given him a fine job. That made him indebted to Jody Simmons no? Very well. He was indebted to Jody Simmons and now he had found a job. How was he to get out of the job Jody Simmons had given him in order to take the new job without offending his benefactor?

All the guys began to get excited. Each one had a different speech he would tell Jody Simmons to get out of the job. One guy thought a good way to do was to punch Jody Simmons right smack in the snoot. Another guy said just to walk in politely and tell Jody Simmons to shove the job up his ass. Another one said just not to show up for work tomorrow and Jody Simmons would catch on real quick. And there were several other ways the guys at the bakery could think of. There ought to have been. They'd been thinking of them for years. A lot of talent had gone to waste thinking of ways to tell Jody Simmons you were quitting. Here was a guy who was actually going to do it so naturally everyone cooperated.

But when all of the solutions had been offered to him Jose shook his head and his eyes looked sadder than ever. He said no he must think of a better way. It would not be gentlemanly to resign in any of the ways suggested. Jody Simmons was his benefactor and one did not do such things to one's benefactor. Even if it were an American custom to do it differently still he would have to follow the customs of his native Porto Rico and in Porto Rico one did not do such things if one were well born.

When you start work on this job Jose? This morning said Jose and I am very tired and now I am going to have to work all night and that will make me much tireder in the morning for the other job and so it will go and it is a terrible problem and I don't know what to do.

So Jose worked all night and the guys in the bakery thought about it and it finally became as puzzling to them as it was to Jose. They would start to think of a way out for Jose and begin to speak and then they would shake their heads and say no that wouldn't do it and then they would go on with

72

their work thinking very hard. This guy Jose was a very queer duck and his ideas were crazy but everybody by this time wanted to find a solution so it became a matter of deep interest to the whole night crew.

The night ended. All the guys in the crew went home and slept and then came back to work that night wondering about Jose. Jose came back too. He was getting pale. He said he was feeling very tired. He said he had gotten only forty-five minutes sleep and that unless he thought of something pretty soon he didn't know what he was going to do. He said surely there must be some American custom to cover his emergency. But they had told him all the American customs the night before and he had turned them down.

So he worked the second night through and when he left in the morning and faced the first glare of sunlight outside the bakery he was a very weak looking man. All the next day he worked for the studio and the next night when he came to work he was almost tottering. He said please please think of some way I can quit this job because a man's health will last only for so long and mine is breaking rapidly since I had no sleep at all today and a man must have sleep if he is going to handle even one job in an honest fashion.

Then Pinky Carson happened to think of something. Jose said Pinky Carson I'll tell you what you do. About two in the morning when the pie run comes down you just pick up six or eight pies in their boxes and walk over in front of where that little window is out of Jody's office so he can see you and you drop those damned pies. Then Jody'll fire you and everything will be all right. Jose thought for a little while. I do not like the use of violence he said finally but I am a desperate man and if you think violence will work I will use it. He thought a little more and then said I can pay for these pies I have violated yes? Everybody said yes if he wanted to be a fool he could pay for the pies he violated.

So that night about two or three o'clock Jose took six pies and stationed himself in the direct line of Jody's vision outside the window of Jody's lean-to office. All the guys were close around looking as if they were working but really watching Jose. They were watching for the minute when Jody Simmons would look out through that window from his desk. When he looked Pinky was to give a signal and then Jose would dump the pies. It seemed that it took Jody longer to look out that window than it ever had before. But finally he did and Pinky Carson gave the signal and Jose dropped the pies.

Jody came zipping out of his office like a bumblebee. He said what the hell is the matter with you you clumsy bastard you turned all these pies over. They're ruined and you'll have to pay for them. Poor Jose stood there almost melting with sadness. He turned his big eyes on Jody Simmons and he said I am so sorry Mister Simmons that I have violated pies. It was an accident I assure you and only a poor workman would have done it and I am miserable about it and I will gladly pay for them and you will accept my apologies yes?

Jody Simmons looked real hard at Jose for a moment and then a smile broke over his face and he said why sure Jose we all make mistakes. You can pay for the pies. He said Jose you are a good conscientious workman and I don't mind if you make a mistake once in a while. He said Jose I wish I had more men like you now forget about the whole thing and go back to work.

Jose stood there kind of quivering all over and shaking his head as if he couldn't believe such bad luck could happen to him. Then he turned and looked at the guys in the crew who had been watching. He looked at Pinky Carson like a dog that has been betrayed by its master. Then he turned and walked over in the first aisle and began to go to work again.

Pinky Carson worked over toward him as soon as possible. Look here Jose he said the idea was all right only it wasn't big enough. To quit a fine job like this you want to do something very big. The pie run is all finished for tonight but don't give up hope Jose because we have a pie run every night and tomorrow you can get one of those big racks of pies. You can get one of those racks that has a hundred and eighty pies just think of it and you can put that rack in the same place and then you can push the rack over and it will make a hell of a mess. Oh boy oh boy what a mess and then Jody Simmons will fire you sure.

Jose looked at Pinky Carson and said the whole thing is very dishonorable but my constitution will not stand very much more so I will do it tomorrow night when the pie run comes. Then he staggered back to his work.

Most of the guys couldn't sleep next day they were so anxious to see Jose dump over that rack. They all came to work early. Jody Simmons didn't get in until around ten o'clock usually. But everybody was hoping he would be in early so they would have a longer time to look at the face of a man who was going to see one hundred and eighty pies turned over right in front of his office. But when they passed Jody's office and looked into it Jody wasn't there. There was nothing but a big long box that looked like a floral box lying on Jody's desk. They all glanced at the box and then went on upstairs and changed for work and pretty soon Jose came in. The first part of the night was the longest any of them ever put in.

About ten o'clock Jody Simmons checked in. Everybody watched because everybody was curious about that box on his desk. Jody walked into the office and stared at the box like it might be a time bomb. He was a very tough man and anything unusual about the place always aroused his suspicions. Finally he must have decided the box was safe because he began to open it very carefully. Two dozen American beauty roses fell out of it onto his desk. Jody began pawing through the roses to find a card but there wasn't any card. When Rudy went into Jody's office to get the night hot sheets he looked at the flowers and said well I see you got some flowers Jody. Jody just glared at the flowers and said that somebody was pulling something funny. But he didn't care because the roses were good and he could take them to his wife. He sent Rudy out to get a can of water to put the roses in so they'd stay fresh. All that night whenever the guys looked toward the little window in Jody's office they saw Jody's bald little head looking as if it wore a wreath of roses.

At two o'clock the pie run began. Pinky Carson

went upstairs to the bakeshop while they were being boxed to check up on them. That night they had apple and vanilla cream and blueberry and peach. Pinky Carson hefted each kind and tested its crust and the thickness of the filling. The crew was well up on its work that night so they could catch the pie run while it was still hot. Pinky Carson decided that the blueberry pies would run the best if they were dumped. So he very carefully picked a rack of the hottest and brought them down on the freight elevator to Jose.

Jose was trembling like a leaf. All the guys stationed near Jody Simmons' window looked like they were working but they were really doing nothing but making motions. Very carefully Pinky worked the pie rack over to the spot in front of Jody Simmons' window. Then he ducked to one side and began making signals to Jose. Jose came up looking like a whipped dog. He went to the pie rack and put his hand up against the back of it. It wouldn't take much of a push to knock it over. Jose stood there just leaning against it and looking sad. Everybody was waiting for Jody Simmons to look out of the window. It seemed like hours. Finally he did and Pinky Carson gave the signal. Jose just pushed a little harder with his hand and the rack went down with a hell of a crash. One hundred and eighty hot blueberry pies spread all over the shipping room floor.

For a minute Jody just sat in his chair and stared. He looked like he couldn't believe a thing like this could ever happen to him. Then it looked like someone gave him an electrical shock because instead of pushing his chair back before getting up he shot straight up like a man on a stove and came running and hollering out of his office. Jose just stood there and looked at him. Jose was much taller than Jody Simmons. He looked down at Jody and his eyes were the saddest things on earth. Jody began screaming at him you lousy spick bastard last night I gave you another chance and tonight what do you do? You smash one hundred and eighty blueberry pies. You know what this means you sonofabitch? This means you're through you're fired get out. Get out and don't ever let me see you again you lousy dirty spick get out.

Jose stood for a minute and looked at Jody Simmons like he was forgiving him for everything he said. Then he turned and walked slowly up to the can. All the guys as quick as they could sneaked up there after him. Jose was almost talking to himself. This is the first time I have ever done anything so dishonorable said Jose. Never have I thought I would stoop to such trickery. Mister Simmons he is quite right. He is a fine gentleman who gave me a job when I was in need. I have repaid him with ingratitude. I am a wretch. There is nothing more to be said no?

Look here Jose said Rudy maybe you know something about those flowers on Jody's desk. Jose nodded. Yes he said but it is what you call it a secret. I have bought the flowers this afternoon and sent them to Mister Simmons. Well you damn fool said Rudy how's he going to know you sent them if you didn't put any name on them?

Jose said that is not a matter for discussion. The important thing is that Mr. Simmons he receives the flowers. Flowers are beautiful. Mister Simmons is a gentleman and he will enjoy them. That he should know where they came from that is quite beside the point. I know that I have expressed my gratitude with something beautiful. I know that I have tried to repay him for the splendid things he has done for me. It is not important that Mr. Simmons he should know it. It is only important that he should receive the roses yes?

Jose put on his coat and walked out of the bakery and nobody ever saw him again. Next day he didn't show up for his check. Instead Jody Simmons received through the mail a money order from Jose for nineteen dollars and eighty-seven cents which with his pay-check would pay for the pies . . .

It seemed that Jose was standing in front of him now weaving back and forth in a kind of fog. He was talking to Jose. He was saying how is everything with you Jose how are you doing? Talk right up Jose and tell me about how you are doing and how you ever came out with that rich girl. Talk louder Jose because I don't seem to be hearing so well lately. Real loud Jose. And come up close because I can't move much. Later on yes but right now you see I'm in bed. How's that Jose how's that?

Jose!

Wait a minute wait a minute Jose. Excuse me. You see I thought we were all in the bakery together again. I thought we were all there. But we're not. I must have been asleep. I must have been dreaming. It's so hard to tell. Just a minute Jose and I'll wake up. There there. That's better much better. I don't know where you are Jose but I know where I am all right.

I know where I am.

He had to stop this. He had to stop things from
fading away and then rushing back at him. He had
to stop the smotherings and the sinkings and the
risings. He had to stop the fear that made him want
to yell and holler and laugh and claw himself to
death with a pair of hands that were rotting in some
hospital dump.

He had to get hold of himself so he could think.
This had been going on too long. His stumps were
healed over now. The bandages were gone. That
meant time had passed. A lot of time. Enough time
so that he had to come out of it and think. He had
to think of himself of Joe Bonham and what he was
going to do next. He had to figure things out all
over again.

It was like a full grown man suddenly being
stuffed back into his mother's body. He was lying in
stillness. He was completely helpless. Somewhere
sticking in his stomach was a tube they fed him

through. That was exactly like the womb except a baby in its mother's body could look forward to the time when it would live.

He would be in this womb forever and ever and ever. He must remember that. He must never expect or hope for anything different. This was his life from now on every day and every hour and every minute of it. He would never again be able to say hello how are you I love you. He would never again be able to hear music or the whisper of the wind through trees or the chuckle of running water. He would never again breathe in the smell of a steak frying in his mother's kitchen or the dampness of springs in the air or the wonderful fragrance of sagebrush carried on the wind across a wide open plain. He would never again be able to see the faces of people who made you glad just to look at them of people like Kareen. He would never again be able to see sunlight or the stars or the little grasses that grow on a Colorado hillside.

He would never walk with his legs on the ground. He would never run or jump or stretch out when he was tired. He would never be tired.

If the place in which he lay were burning he would simply stay there and let it burn. He would burn up with it and not be able to make a move. If he should feel an insect crawling over the stump of body that remained he could not move one finger to destroy it. If it stung him he could do nothing to ease the itch except maybe to writhe a little against his covers. And this life wouldn't last only today or tomorrow or until the end of next week. He was in his womb forever. It wasn't any dream. It was real.

He wondered how he could have come through it

alive. You heard about somebody scratching his thumb and the next thing you knew he was dead. The mountain climber fell off the front stoop and fractured his skull and died by Thursday. Your best friend went to the hospital to have his appendix taken out and four or five days later you were standing beside his grave. A little germ like influenza carried off five maybe ten million people in a single winter. Then how could a guy lose his arms and legs and ears and eyes and nose and mouth and still be alive? How did you make any sense out of it?

Still there were plenty of people who had lost just their legs or just their arms and were living. So maybe it was reasonable to think that a man could live all right if he lost both his legs and his arms. If one was possible probably both were possible. The doctors were getting pretty smart especially now that they had had three or four years in the army with plenty of raw material to experiment on. If they got to you quickly enough so you didn't bleed to death they could save you from almost any kind of injury. Evidently they had got to him quickly enough.

It was fairly reasonable when you thought of it. Plenty guys had their hearing smashed from concussion. Nothing unusual about that. Lots of guys had been blinded. You even read in the papers once in a while about somebody trying to put a bullet through his temple and ending up healthy except he was blind. So his blindness made sense too. There were plenty guys in hospitals back of the lines who were breathing through tubes and plenty without chins and plenty without noses. The whole thing made sense. Only he had combined them all. The shell had simply scooped out his whole face and the doctors had got to him soon enough to keep him from bleeding to death. Just a nice clean slice of the shell that somehow missed his jugular vein and his spine.

Things had been pretty quiet for a while just before he got his. That meant the doctors in back of the lines had more time to play with him than during an offensive when guys were being brought in by the truckload. That must be it. They had picked him up quickly and hauled him back to a base hospital and all of them had rolled up their sleeves and rubbed their hands together and said well boys here's a very interesting problem let's see what we can do. After all they'd only carved up ten thousand guys back there learning how. Now they had come upon something that was a challenge and they had plenty of time so they fixed him up and tucked him back into the womb.

But why hadn't he bled to death? You'd think that with the stumps of two arms and two legs spouting blood a man could at least die. There were some mighty big veins in your legs and arms. He'd seen guys bleed to death from losing just an arm. It didn't seem reasonable the doctors could work fast enough to stop all four flows at once before a man died. Then he thought maybe I was only wounded in them just wounded a little and they were cut off later maybe to save trouble or maybe because they were infected. He remembered stories of gangrene and of soldiers found with their wounds filled with maggots. That was a very good sign. If you had a bullet in your stomach and a hole was squirming alive with maggots then you were all right because the maggots ate away the pus and kept the wound clean. But if you had the same hole and no maggots you simply festered for a while and then you had gangrene.

Perhaps he had had no maggots. Maybe if he had been able to scare up just a handful of little white worms he might right now have legs and arms. Just a handful of little white worms. Perhaps when he had been picked up he still had his legs and arms with only a few wounds in them. But by the time they got the important things like his eyes and nose and ears and mouth fixed up the gangrene had started in his legs and arms. Then they started hacking. A toe here a wrist joint there oh hell let's take it off at the hip. That was probably the way. When doctors are only chopping things off they have ways of stopping the blood so that a man doesn't necessarily die from loss of it. Maybe if the doctors had known how he would end up they would have let him die. But it happened gradually joint by joint and so here he was alive and they couldn't kill him now because that would be murder.

Oh hell there were a lot of funny things happened in this man's war. Anything could be true. You heard about them all the time. One guy had the whole top of his stomach shot away so they took skin and meat from a dead man and they made a flap over the first guy's stomach. They could lift the flap like a window and watch him digest his food. There were whole rooms filled with men who breathed through tubes and other wards where men ate through tubes and would eat through them the rest of their lives. Tubes were important. Lots of guys would piss through tubes as long as they lived

and there were plenty who had had their rear ends
shot off. Now their bowels were connected up with
holes in their sides or stomachs. The holes were covered with absorbent bandages because they had no
muscles there to control themselves.

And that wasn't all. There was a place in South-
ern France where they kept the crazy ones. There
were guys who couldn't talk even though they were
in perfect shape. They had just got scared and had
forgotten how to talk. There were healthy able
bodied men who ran around on all fours and stuck
their heads in corners when they were frightened
and smelled each other and lifted their legs like
dogs and couldn't do anything but whimper. There
was a guy a coal miner went back to his wife and
three kids in Cardiff. His face had been burned off
by a flare one night and when his wife saw him she
let out a screech and grabbed a hatchet and chopped
his head off and then killed the three kids. They
found her drinking beer just as cool as a cucumber
down in a saloon that same night. Only thing was
she was trying to eat the glass the beer came in.
How could you believe or disbelieve anything any
more? Four maybe five million men killed and none
of them wanting to die while hundreds maybe thousands were left crazy or blind or crippled and couldn't
die no matter how hard they tried.

But there weren't many like him. There weren't
many guys the doctors could point to and say here
is the last word here is our triumph here is the
greatest thing we ever did and we did plenty. Here
is a man without legs or arms or ears or eyes or
nose or mouth who breathes and eats and is just as
alive as you or me. The war had been a wonderful

thing for the doctors and he was the lucky guy who had profited by everything they learned. But there was one thing they couldn't do. They might be perfectly able to put a guy back into the womb but they couldn't get him out again. He was there for good. All the parts that were gone from him were gone forever. That was the thing he must remember. That was the thing he must try to believe. When that sank in he could calm down and think.

It was like reading in the paper that someone has won a lottery and saying to yourself there's a guy who won a million to one shot. You never quite believed that a man could win against such odds yet you knew he had. Certainly you never expected to win yourself even if you bought a ticket. Now he was just the reverse. He had lost a million to one shot. Yet if he read about himself in a newspaper he wouldn't be able to believe it even though he knew it was true. And he would never expect it to happen to him. Nobody expected it. But he could believe anything from now on out. A million to one ten million to one there was always the one. And he was it. He was the guy who had lost.

He was beginning to quiet down now. His thoughts were coming through a little clearer a little more connectedly. He could lie here against his sheet and put things together. He could figure out the small things that were wrong with him in addition to the great. Down somewhere near the base of his throat there was a scab that was sticking to something. By tossing his head slightly to the right and then to the left he could feel the pull of the scab. He could also feel a little tug at his forehead as if a cord had been tied around there halfway between his eye sockets and his hairline. He began to puzzle about the cord and why it pulled when he tossed his head to get the feel of the scab near his neck. In the hole which was the middle of his face he could feel nothing so it made a nice little problem. He lay there tossing to the right tossing to the left feeling the pressure and feeling the scab pull. Then he got it.

They had put a mask over his face and it was tied at the top around his forehead. The mask was evidently some sort of soft cloth and the lower part of it had stuck to the raw mucus of his face wound. That explained the whole thing. The mask was just a square of cloth tied securely and pulled down toward his throat so that the nurse in her comings and goings wouldn't vomit at the sight of her patient. It was a very thoughtful arrangement.

Now that he understood the purpose and mechanics of the mask the scab became an irritation instead of merely a curious thing. Even when he was a kid he could never let a scab quite heal over. He was always picking at it. Now he was picking at this scab by tossing his head and drawing the mask tight. But he couldn't dislodge the mask or start the scab to peeling. The task became a kind of mania with him. The place where the cloth stuck to the scab didn't hurt. It wasn't that. But the whole thing was an annoyance and a challenge and an issue of strength. If he could dislodge the mask then he was not completely helpless.

He tried to stretch his neck so he could rip the cloth from the flesh. But he couldn't stretch far enough. He found himself concentrating all his energy and all his mind on that tiny point of irritation. And then tug by tug he realized he would never

87

be able to dislodge it. Just so small a thing as a piece of cloth stuck to his skin yet all the muscles of his body and all the power of his brain couldn't budge it. That was worse than being in the womb. Babies sometimes kicked. They sometimes turned over in their dark silent watery resting places. But he had no legs to kick with and no arms to thrash with and he couldn't turn over because he had no leverage in his body to start him rolling. He tried to shift his weight from side to side but the muscles in what was left of his thighs wouldn't flex properly and his shoulders were cut down so narrowly that they weren't any good either.

He abandoned the scab and the mask and began to scheme about turning over. He could produce a faint rocking motion but nothing more. Perhaps with practice he might increase the strength of his back and thighs and shoulders. Perhaps after one or five or twenty years he could develop such strength that the circle of his rocking would become wider and wider and wider. And then one day flip-flop and he'd be turned over. If he could do this he might be able to kill himself because if the tubes which fed his lungs and stomach were of metal the weight of his body might plunge the metal into some vital organ. Or if they were soft like rubber his weight would shut them off and he would suffocate.

But all he could get out of his most violent efforts was that faint rocking motion and even to produce that made him wet with sweat and dizzy from pain. He was twenty years old and he couldn't even summon enough strength to turn over in bed. He had never been sick a day in his life. He had always been strong. He had been able to lift a box packed with sixty loaves of bread with each loaf weighing a pound and a half. He had been able to throw such a box over his shoulder and on top of a seven foot route bin without even thinking of it. He had been able to do this not only once but hundreds of times each night until his shoulders and biceps were hard as iron. And now he could only flex his thighs weakly and make a little rolling motion like a child rocking itself to sleep.

Suddenly he was very tired. He lay back quietly and thought about that other that minor injury he had begun to notice. There was a hole in his side. It was just a small hole but evidently it wouldn't heal. His legs and arms were healed and that took a lot of time. But during all that time of healing during all those weeks or months when he had been fainting in and out of things the hole in his side had remained open. He had been noticing it little by little for a long while and now he could feel it plainly. It was a patch of moisture inside a bandage and from it moisture was slipping down his left side in a slick little trail.

He remembered the time he visited Jim Tift at the military hospital in Lille. Jim had been put in a ward where there were a lot of guys who had holes here and there that wouldn't heal. Some of them had been lying there draining and stinking for months. The smell of that ward when you hit it was like the smell of a corpse you stumble over on patrol duty like the smell of a rich ripe corpse that falls open at the touch of a boot and sends up a stench of dead flesh like a cloud of gas.

Maybe he was lucky his nose was shot off. It would be pretty bad to have to lie and smell the perfume of your own body as it rotted away. Maybe he was a lucky guy after all because with a smell like that constantly in your nose you wouldn't have much of an appetite. But then that wouldn't bother him anyhow. He ate regular. He could feel them sliding stuff into his belly and he knew he was eating all right. Flavor didn't matter to him.

Things were getting dimmer and dimmer now. He knew he wasn't fainting again. He was slipping away. It seemed that the blackness in his eyes was changing to something purple something like twilight blue. He was resting. He was simply lying back after a lot of thinking and hard work and saying let it run let it fester because I can't smell it anyhow. When you have so little left why should you care if part of it is dying? You lie back. The darkness changes to another shade of darkness. Starless twilight and starless night. Like at home. Like at home in the evenings with crickets and frogs and a cow lowing somewhere and a dog barking way off and the sounds of children playing. Wonderful beautiful sounds and darkness and peace and sleep. Only no stars.

The rat came crawling over him stealthily. It came with its sharp little claws up his left leg. It was a great brown trench rat like the ones they used to throw shovels at. It came crawling and sniffing and smelling and tearing away at the bandage over his side. He could feel its whiskers as they tickled the edges of the draining wound. He could feel its long whiskers as they trailed in the pus from the hole. And there was nothing he could do about it.

He remembered the face of a Prussian officer they discovered one day. They had just stormed the outer

90

trenches of the German position. It was a trench that had been abandoned a week maybe two weeks before. They all swarmed into it a whole company on their way forward. There they came upon the Prussian officer. He was a captain. He was lying with one leg straight up in the air. The leg was swelled so much the pants looked as if they were ready to bust open. His face was swelled too. His moustache was still waxed. Sitting on his neck and chewing away at his face was a fat contented rat. As they came jumping over into the trench they got the whole picture. The entrance to a dugout toward which the Prussian had been heading when he was hit. The Prussian with his leg up in the air. The rat chewing.

Somebody let out a yell and then they were all yelling like crazy men. The rat sat up and looked at him. Then the rat started for the dugout entrance. But he started too slow. Yelling and screaming the whole pack of them were after him. Somebody ripped off a helmet and it hit the rat in its hind-quarters. The rat squealed and turned to snap at the helmet. Then it dragged itself into the dugout with all of them after it. They caught it there in the dim light and beat it into red jelly. Then they were all still for a second. They felt kind of foolish. They left the dugout and went on with the war.

He thought about it afterward. It didn't matter whether the rat was gnawing on your buddy or a damned German it was all the same. Your real enemy was the rat and when you saw it there fat and well fed chewing on something that might be you why you went nuts.

The rat was eating on him now. He could feel its

sharp little teeth as they bit into the edge of the wound and then he could feel the quick little movements through the rat's body as it chewed. Then it would dig its feet in and scoop out a bit more of flesh and that would hurt and then it would chew again.

He wondered where the nurse was. It was a hell of a hospital where they let rats come right into the wards and chew the customers while they were trying to get some sleep. He wiggled and twisted but the rat hung on tight. There wasn't anything he could do to scare it. He couldn't hit it or kick at it and he couldn't yell or whistle to frighten it. The only thing he could do was to go into that slow rocking motion. But the rat evidently liked that because it stayed right where it was. The rat was eating very carefully now taking only the choicest parts and then squatting flat on its stomach with its little jaws chewing chewing chewing.

He began to realize that the chewing of the rat was not a thing that would last only for ten or fifteen minutes. Rats were smart animals. They knew their way around. This one wouldn't be content to go away and not come back again. It would return from day to day and from night to night to feed at his carcass until he went crazy. He found himself running through the corridors of the hospital. He found himself coming upon a nurse and grabbing her by the throat and putting her head down to the hole in his side where the rat was still clinging and hollering at her you lazy slut why don't you come and chase the rats off your customers? He was running through the night shrieking. Running through a whole series of nights running through an eternity of nights yelling for Christ sake somebody take this rat off me see him hanging there? Running through a lifetime of nights and shrieking and trying to push the rat off and feeling the rat sink its teeth deeper and deeper.

When he had run without legs until he was tired and when he had screamed without voice until his throat hurt he fell back into the womb back into the quietude back into the loneliness and the blackness and the terrible silence.

The nurse's hands were on him. He could feel her washing his body and manipulating his flesh and dressing the wound in his side. She used something warm and greasy to dissolve the scab substance that held the mask to that point of irritation near his throat. He felt like a child that has awakened weeping from a nightmare to find itself safe and snug in its mother's arms. The nurse was company even though he couldn't see or hear her. She was somebody and she was his friend. He wasn't alone any longer. With her at hand there was no need for him to worry no need for him to struggle no need for him to think. The responsibility was completely hers and he had nothing to fear so long as she was close to him. Instead of the rat gnawing at his side he felt her cool fingers and the cleanliness of new bandages and fresh linen.

He knew now that the rat had been only a dream. He was so relieved to discover this that for a few minutes he almost forgot his fear. And then relaxing under the nurse's care he suddenly chilled all over at realization that the rat dream might come again. It was almost a certainty to come again. He knew that the whole dream was started by his thinking of the wound in his side. His awareness of the wound as he fell asleep brought on the dream of the rat feeding at it. Since the wound remained it seemed almost certain that the same chain of thought would bring the rat back to him again in his sleep. Each time he fell asleep the rat would come and sleep instead of being forgetfulness would become as bad as being awake. A guy could stand a lot when he was awake. But when sleep came he deserved to forget everything. Sleep should be like death.

He knew the rat was a dream. He was sure of that. All he had to do was to find some way of getting himself out of the dream when it came. He could remember when he was a kid he used to have nightmares. Funny thing about them was they weren't particularly awful ones either. The worst one was where he seemed to be an ant walking across a sidewalk and the sidewalk was so big and he was so small that sometimes he awakened yelling he was so scared. That was the way to stop nightmares by yelling so hard you waked yourself up. But hell that wouldn't work for him now. In the first place he couldn't yell and in the second place he was so deaf he couldn't hear the noise anyhow. That was no good. He would have to find some other way.

He remembered that as he got older and different nightmares came he used to be able to think himself out of them. Just when it seemed the awful thing that was after him was going to get him he could think in his sleep here Joe this is just a dream. It's just a dream Joe understand? And then in a little bit he would open his eyes and look into the darkness around him and the dream would be gone. That system might work with the rat. Instead of imagining himself running and yelling for help the next time the rat came he would just think to himself this is a dream. And then he would open—

But that wouldn't work. He couldn't open his eyes. In his sleep in the middle of the rat dream he might think himself out of it but how would he be able to prove he was awake if he couldn't open his eyes and look around into the darkness?

He thought Jesus Joe there must be some other way. He thought it's asking very little for a man just to want to be able to prove that he's awake. He thought come on Joe this is the only way you can lick the rat and you've got to do that so you'd better figure out some way quick to prove whether you're awake or asleep.

Maybe he'd better start from the beginning. He was awake now. He was sure of that. He had just felt the nurse's hands and the nurse's hands were real. So when he felt them he was awake. Even though the nurse was gone now he was still awake because he was thinking about the rat dream. If you're thinking about a dream that's proof you're awake. That's clear enough Joe. You're awake. And you're trying to get rid of a dream that will come when you go to sleep. You can't wake yourself out of your sleep by yelling because you can't yell. You can't think yourself out of it and then prove it's gone by opening your eyes because you haven't got any eyes. Better start in before you go to sleep Joe that's the business start in right now.

The minute you feel sleepy like you're going to topple off why just kind of stiffen yourself and tell yourself that you're not going to have any dreams about rats. Then maybe you'll be so ready for it that it won't come. Because once it comes it's got you till you wake up and you can't be sure that you're awake until you feel the nurse's hands. You can't be absolutely sure till then. So when you feel like you're getting sleepy you just think hard that you're not going to dream about the—

Hold on there. How're you going to know when you begin to feel sleepy Joe? What's going to tell you that you're sleepy? Just how does a guy feel before he topples off to sleep? Well maybe he's all tired out from working and he just relaxes in bed and the first thing he knows he's asleep. But that's no good for you Joe because you never get that tired and you're in bed all the time. That's no good. Well then maybe his eyes burn a little and he yawns and stretches and finally his lids drop down. But that's no good either. Your eyes don't ever burn and you can't yawn and stretch and you've got no eyelids. You're never tired Joe. You don't need any sleep because you're practically sleeping all the time. So how can you get sleepy? If you can't get sleepy you've got no warning. And if you've got no warning you can't stiffen yourself in advance against the rat.

Jesus he was in an awful mess. He was in an awful mess if he couldn't even tell whether he was awake or asleep. But there wasn't any way to tell he could think of. When you're going to sleep you're tired and you lie down and you close your eyes and sound dies away and then you're asleep. Maybe even a normal guy a guy with eyes to close and ears to hear with can't tell the actual minute he falls asleep. Maybe nobody can. There's a little space between being awake and being asleep that isn't either one. The two things just melt together so that without knowing it you're asleep. And then without realizing that you're waking up all of a sudden you're awake.

It was a hell of a thing. If even a normal guy couldn't tell how was he going to tell when everything about him was like sleep all the time twenty four hours a day? For all he knew he might be slipping in and out of sleep every five minutes or so. His whole life was so much like sleep that he had no way of keeping track. Of course it stood to reason that he was awake a lot of the time. But the only time he could be positive he was awake was when he felt the nurse's hands. And now that he knew the rat was a dream and since it was the only dream he could absolutely tie down why the only time he could be sure he was asleep was when the rat was gnawing. Of course he might have other dreams beside the rat just as he might be awake lots of times when the nurse's hands weren't touching him. But how in the hell could he tell?

For example when he was a kid he used to day dream. He used to sit back and think of things he'd do some day. Or he used to think of things he did last week. But all the time he would be awake. He knew that. Yet with him lying here in bed in blackness and silence it was different. In thinking over something that happened a long while ago what seemed like a day dream might become a real dream so that as he thought of the past he fell asleep and dreamed about it.

Maybe there wasn't any way. Maybe for the rest of his life he would just have to guess whether he was awake or asleep. How was he ever going to be able to say well I guess I'll go to sleep now or I just woke up? How was he going to know? And a guy had to know. That was important. It was the most important thing left. All he had was a mind and he would like to feel that it was thinking clearly. But how was he going to do it except when there was a nurse at hand or a rat on him?

He had to do it that was all. Guys were supposed to develop extra powers when they lost parts of themselves. Maybe if he concentrated on thinking he would know he was awake just like he knew he was awake now. Then when he stopped concentrating he would know he was going to fall asleep. That meant no more dreaming about the past. That meant no more of anything but thinking thinking thinking. Then he'd get so tired of thinking that he'd be drowsy and he'd fall asleep. He had a mind left by god and that was all. It was the only thing he could use so he must use it every minute he was awake. He must think till he was tired tireder than he had ever been before. He must think all the time and then he must sleep.

He saw he had to do it. Because if he couldn't tell being awake from being asleep why he couldn't even consider himself a grown-up person. It was bad enough to be shot back into the womb. It was bad enough to think of going on for years and years in loneliness and silence and blackness. But this latest thing his inability to tell dreams from thoughts was oblivion. It made him nothing and less than nothing. It robbed him of the only thing that distinguished a normal person from a crazy man. It meant that he might be lying and thinking very solemnly about something that seemed important while all the time he might really be asleep and dreaming the idiotic dreams of a two year old. It robbed him of any respect for his own thoughts and that was the worst thing that could happen to anybody. He was so mixed up that he wasn't sure whether the nurse or the rat was real. Maybe neither was real. Maybe both were real. Maybe nothing was real not even himself oh god and wouldn't that be wonderful.

The campfire was built in front of a tent and the tent was under an enormous pine. When you slept inside the tent it seemed always that it was raining outside because the needles from the pine kept falling. Sitting across from him and staring into the fire was his father. Each summer they came to this place which was nine thousand feet high and covered with pine trees and dotted with lakes. They fished in the lakes and when they slept at night the roar of water from the streams which connected the lakes sounded in their ears all night long.

They had been coming to this place ever since he was seven. Now he was fifteen and Bill Harper was going to come tomorrow. He sat in front of the fire and looked across at his father and wondered just how he was going to tell him. It was a very serious thing. Tomorrow for the first time in all their trips together he wanted to go fishing with someone other than his father. On previous trips the idea had never occurred to him. His father had always preferred his company to that of men and he had always preferred his father's company to that of the other guys. But now Bill Harper was coming up tomorrow and he wanted to go fishing with him. He knew it was something that had to happen sometime. Yet he also knew that it was the end of something. It was an ending and a beginning and he wondered just how he should tell his father about it.

So he told him very casually. He said Bill Harper's coming up tomorrow and I thought maybe I'd go out with him. He said Bill Harper doesn't know very much about fishing and I do so I think if you don't mind I'll get up early in the morning and meet Harper and he and I will go fishing.

For a little while his father didn't say a thing. Then he said why sure go along Joe. And then a little later his father said has Bill Harper got a rod? He told his father no Bill hasn't a rod. Well said his father why don't you take my rod and let Bill use yours? I don't want to go fishing tomorrow anyhow. I'm tired and I think I'll rest all day. So you use my rod and let Bill use yours.

It was as simple as that and yet he knew it was a great thing. His father's rod was a very valuable one. It was perhaps the only extravagance his father had had in his whole life. It had amber leaders and beautiful silk windings. Each spring his father sent the rod away to a man in Colorado Springs who was an expert on rods. The man in Colorado Springs carefully scraped the varnish off the rod and rewound it and revarnished it and it came back glistening new each year. There was nothing his father treasured more. He felt a little lump in his throat as he thought that even as he was deserting his father for Bill Harper his father had volunteered the rod.

They went to sleep that night in the bed which lay against a floor of pine needles. They had scooped the needles out to make a little hollow place for their hips. He lay awake quite a while thinking about tomorrow and his father who slept beside him. Then he fell asleep. At six o'clock Bill Harper whispered to him through the tent flap. He got up and gave Bill his rod and took his father's for himself and they went off without awakening his father.

It was growing dark when the terrible thing happened. They were in a rowboat trolling with spinners. They had both lines out. He was rowing and Bill Harper was at the stern sitting down facing him and holding a rod out on each side of the boat. It was very quiet and the lake was glassy still. They were both feeling a little dreamy because they had had such a wonderful time all day. Then there was a sharp whirring sound as the fish struck. The rod leaped out of Bill Harper's hand and disappeared into the water. Both of them made wild grabs for it but they were too late. It was his father's rod. They fished around for more than an hour with the other rod and with the oars of the boat hoping to raise it but they knew all the while there was no chance. His father's wonderful rod was gone and they would never see it again.

They beached the boat and cleaned the fish they had caught and then they went over to the general store for a root beer. They drank their root beer and talked in hushed tones about the rod. Then he left Bill Harper.

All the way to the tent walking under pine trees

and over soft needle carpets and hearing the sound of the streams rushing down the mountain and seeing the stars in the sky he thought about his father. His father and mother never had much money but they seemed to get along all right. They had a little house set far back on a long wide lot near the edge of town. In front of the house there was a space of lawn and between the lawn and the sidewalk his father had a lot of room for gardening. People would come from all over town to admire his father's garden. His father would get up at five or five-thirty in the mornings to go out and irrigate the garden. He would come home from work in the evenings eager to return to it. The garden in a way was his father's escape from bills and success stories and the job at the store. It was his father's way of creating something. It was his father's way of being an artist.

At first they had lettuce and beans and peas and carrots and onions and beets and radishes. Then his father got consent from the man who owned the vacant lot next door to use the lot for gardening space also. The man was glad enough to have his father use it because it would save him the expense of burning the weeds off in the fall. So on the vacant lot his father raised sweet corn and summer squash and cantaloupes and watermelons and cucumbers. He had a great hedge of sunflowers around it. The sunflower hearts were sometimes a foot across. The seeds made fine food for the chickens. In a little patch that had shade half the day his father planted everbearing strawberries so they had fresh berries from spring until late fall.

In back of the house in Shale City they had chickens and rabbits and he had some bantams for pets.

Two maybe three times a week they had fried chicken for dinner and it didn't seem like a luxury. In the winter they had stewing hens with dumplings and potatoes from their own vines. During the season when the chickens laid a lot of eggs and eggs were cheap at the store his mother took the extra eggs from the henhouse and put them up in big crocks of waterglass. Then when winter came and eggs were expensive and the hens weren't laying she just went down into the cellar and got her eggs for nothing. They kept a cow and his mother churned their own butter and they had buttermilk. The milk set in pans on the back porch and in the morning the milk from the night before was covered with yellow cream almost as heavy as leather. On hot summer Sundays they made ice cream using their own cream and their own strawberries and practically everything else their own except the ice.

On the far side of the vacant lot his father had six stands of bees so that every fall they had plenty of honey. His father would go out to the bee stands and pull out the sections and check on the cells and if the stand was weak he would destroy all the queen cells and perhaps even clip the queen's wings so that she wouldn't swarm and split the hive.

As soon as the weather got below freezing his father went out to some nearby farmer's and bought fresh meat. There would be a quarter of beef and maybe half a hog hanging on the back porch frozen through and always fresh. When you wanted a steak you simply took a saw and you sawed the steak off and besides being better it didn't cost you anything like the butcher shops charged.

In the fall his mother spent weeks canning fruit.

By the end of the season the cellar was packed. You would go down there and beside the great crocks of water-glassed eggs there would be mason jars of every kind of fruit you could want. There would be apricot preserves and orange marmalade and raspberry jam and blueberry jam and apple jelly. There would be hard-boiled eggs canned in beet juice and bread and butter pickles and salted cherries and chili sauce. If you went down in October you would find three or four heavy fruit cakes black and moist and filled with citron and nuts. They would be in the coolest corner of the cellar and they would be carefully wrapped with damp cloths against the Christmas season.

All of these things they had and yet his father was a failure. His father couldn't make any money. Sometimes his father and mother talked together in the evenings about it. So-and-so had gone to California and had made a lot of money in real estate. So-and-so had gone and made a lot of money just by working in a chain shoe store until he got to be manager. Everybody who went to California made money and was a success. But his father in Shale City was a failure.

It was hard to understand how his father could be such a big failure when you stopped to think about the thing. He was a good man and an honest man. He kept his children together and they ate good food fine food rich food better food than people ate in the cities. Even rich people in the cities couldn't get vegetables as fresh or as crisp. They couldn't get meat as well cured. No amount of money could buy that. Those things you had to raise for yourself. His father had managed to do it even to the honey they used on the hot biscuits his mother made. His father had managed to produce all these things on two city lots and yet his father was a failure.

He saw the tent rising ahead of him out of the mountainside like a small white cloud in the darkness. He thought about the rod again and then he knew why his father was a failure. It wasn't that his father didn't provide for his family and keep them in clothes and food and pleasures. It was all very plain now. His father didn't have enough money to buy another rod. Even though the rod was his father's most cherished possession now that it was gone he wouldn't have enough money to buy another and so he was a failure.

When he got to the tent his father was in bed and asleep. He stood for a minute looking down at his father. Then he went out and strung up his fish. He returned to the tent and undressed quickly and got into bed beside his father. His father stirred. He knew it was no good waiting till morning. He had to tell his father now. His voice wouldn't come clearly when he began to talk. It wasn't because he was afraid of what his father might say. It was because he knew that his father would never again be able to have a rod as good as the one that was gone.

Dad he said we lost your rod. We got a quick strike and before we knew it the rod was in the water. We hunted around for it and fished with the oars but we didn't get it so it's lost.

It seemed like maybe five minutes before his father made a sound. Then he turned slightly over in bed. He felt his father's arm suddenly thrown over his chest. He felt its warm comforting pressure. Well said his father I don't think we should let a little thing like a fishing rod spoil our last trip together should we?

There was nothing to say so he just lay still. His father had known all along that it was really their last trip together. From now on in the summers he would come up camping with guys like Bill Harper and Glen Hogan and the rest of them. And his father would come on fishing trips with men. It had just happened that way. It had to happen that way. But he lay there in bed beside his father with the two of them jack-knifed together in the way they always slept best and his father's arm around him and he blinked back the tears. He and his father had lost everything. Themselves and the rod.

He awakened thinking of his father and wondering where the nurse was. He awakened lonelier than he had been since he could remember. He was lonely for Shale City and its pleasant ways. He was lonely for one look for one smell for one taste for one word that would bring Shale City and his father and his mother and his sisters back to him. But he was so cut off from them that even if they were standing beside his bed they would be as distant as if they were ten thousand miles away.

Lying on your back without anything to do and anywhere to go was kind of like being on a high hill far away from noise and people. It was like being on a camping trip all by yourself. You had plenty of time to think. You had time to figure things out. Things you'd never thought of before. Things like for example going to war. You were so completely alone on your hill that noise and people didn't enter in your figuring of things at all. You figured only for yourself without considering a single little thing outside yourself. It seemed that you thought clearer and that your answers made more sense. And even if they didn't make sense it didn't matter because you weren't ever going to be able to do anything about them anyhow.

He thought here you are Joe Bonham lying like a side of beef all the rest of your life and for what? Somebody tapped you on the shoulder and said come along son we're going to war. So you went.

But why? In any other deal even like buying a car or running an errand you had the right to say what's there in it for me? Otherwise you'd be buying bad cars for too much money or running errands for fools and starving to death. It was a kind of duty you owed yourself that when anybody said come on son do this or do that you should stand up and say look mister why should I do this for who am I doing it and what am I going to get out of it in the end? But when a guy comes along and says here come with me and risk your life and maybe die or be crippled why then you've got no rights. You haven't even the right to say yes or no or I'll think it over. There are plenty of laws to protect guys' money even in war time but there's nothing on the books says a man's life's his own.

Of course a lot of guys were ashamed. Somebody said let's go out and fight for liberty and so they went and got killed without ever once thinking about liberty. And what kind of liberty were they fighting for anyway? How much liberty and whose idea of liberty? Were they fighting for the liberty of eating free ice cream cones all their lives or for the liberty of robbing anybody they pleased whenever they wanted to or what? You tell a man he can't rob and you take away some of his liberty. You've got to. What the hell does liberty mean anyhow? It's just a word like house or table or any other word. Only it's a special kind of word. A guy says house and he can point to a house to prove it. But a guy says come on let's fight for liberty and he can't show you liberty. He can't prove the thing he's talking about so how in the hell can he be telling you to fight for it?

No sir anybody who went out and got into the

front line trenches to fight for liberty was a goddam
fool and the guy who got him there was a liar. Next
time anybody came gabbling to him about liberty—
what did he mean next time? There wasn't going to
be any next time for him. But the hell with that. If
there could be a next time and somebody said let's
fight for liberty he would say mister my life is important. I'm not a fool and when I swap my life for
liberty I've got to know in advance what liberty is
and whose idea of liberty we're talking about and
just how much of that liberty we're going to have.
And what's more mister are you as much interested
in this liberty as you want me to be? And maybe too
much liberty will be as bad as too little liberty and I
think you're a goddam fourflusher talking through
your hat and I've already decided that I like the liberty I've got right here the liberty to walk and see
and hear and talk and eat and sleep with my girl. I
think I like that liberty better than fighting for a lot
of things we won't get and ending up without any
liberty at all. Ending up dead and rotting before my
life is even begun good or ending up like a side of
beef. Thank you mister. You fight for liberty. Me I
don't care for some.

Hell's fire guys had always been fighting for liberty. America fought a war for liberty in 1776. Lots
of guys died. And in the end does America have any
more liberty than Canada or Australia who didn't
fight at all? Maybe so I'm not arguing I'm just asking. Can you look at a guy and say he's an American
who fought for his liberty and anybody can see he's
a very different guy from a Canadian who didn't? No
by god you can't and that's that. So maybe a lot of
guys with wives and kids died in 1776 when they

didn't need to die at all. They're dead now anyway. Sure but that doesn't do any good. A guy can think of being dead a hundred years from now and he doesn't mind it. But to think of being dead tomorrow morning and to be dead forever to be nothing but dust and stink in the earth is that liberty?

They were always fighting for something the bastards and if anyone dared say the hell with fighting it's all the same each war is like the other and nobody gets any good out of it why they hollered coward. If they weren't fighting for liberty they were fighting for independence or democracy or freedom or decency or honor or their native land or something else that didn't mean anything. The war was to make the world safe for democracy for the little countries for everybody. If the war was over now then the world must be all safe for democracy. Was it? And what kind of democracy? And how much? And whose?

Then there was this freedom the little guys were always getting killed for. Was it freedom from another country? Freedom from work or disease or death? Freedom from your mother-in-law? Please mister give us a bill of sale on this freedom before we go out and get killed. Give us a bill of sale drawn up plainly so we know in advance what we're getting killed for and give us also a first mortgage on something as security so we can be sure after we've won your war that we've got the same kind of freedom we bargained for.

And take decency. Everybody said America was fighting a war for the triumph of decency. But whose idea of decency? And decency for who? Speak up and tell us what decency is. Tell us how much better a decent dead man feels that an indecent live one. Make a comparison there in facts like houses and tables. Make it in words we can understand. And don't talk about honor. The honor of a Chinese or an Englishman or an African negro or an American or a Mexican? Please all you guys who want to fight to preserve our honor let us know what the hell honor is. Is it American honor for the whole world we're fighting for? Maybe the world doesn't like it. Maybe the South Sea Islanders like their honor better.

For Christ sake give us things to fight for we can see and feel and pin down and understand. No more highfalutin words that mean nothing like native land. Motherland fatherland homeland native land. It's all the same. What the hell good to you is your native land after you're dead? Whose native land is it after you're dead? If you get killed fighting for your native land you've bought a pig in a poke. You've paid for something you'll never collect.

And when they couldn't hook the little guys into fighting for liberty or freedom or democracy or independence or decency or honor they tried the women. Look at the dirty Huns they would say look at them how they rape the beautiful French and Belgian girls. Somebody's got to stop all that raping. So come on little guy join the army and save the beautiful French and Belgian girls. So the little guy got bewildered and he signed up and in a little while a shell hit him and his life spattered out of him in red meat pulp and he was dead. Dead for another word and all the fierce old bats of the D.A.R. get out and hurrah themselves hoarse over his grave because he died for womanhood.

Now it might be that a guy would risk getting killed if his women were being raped. But if he did why he was only striking a bargain. He was simply saying that according to the way he felt at the time the safety of his women was worth more than his own life. But there wasn't anything particularly noble or heroic about it. It was a straight deal his life for something he valued more. It was more or less like any other deal a man might make. But when you change your women to all the women in the world why you begin to defend women in the bulk. To do that you have to fight in the bulk. And by that time you're fighting for a word again.

When armies begin to move and flags wave and slogans pop up watch out little guy because it's somebody else's chestnuts in the fire not yours. It's words you're fighting for and you're not making an honest deal your life for something better. You're being noble and after you're killed the thing you traded your life for won't do you any good and chances are it won't do anybody else any good either.

Maybe that's a bad way to think. There are lots of idealists around who will say have we got so low that nothing is more precious than life? Surely there are ideals worth fighting for even dying for. If not then we are worse than the beasts of the field and have sunk into barbarity. Then you say that's all right let's be barbarous just so long as we don't have war. You keep your ideals just as long as they don't cost me my life. And they say but surely life isn't as important as principle. Then you say oh no? Maybe not yours but mine is. What the hell is principle? Name it and you can have it.

You can always hear the people who are willing

to sacrifice somebody else's life. They're plenty loud and they talk all the time. You can find them in churches and schools and newspapers and legislatures and congress. That's their business. They sound wonderful. Death before dishonor. This ground sanctified by blood. These men who died so gloriously. They shall not have died in vain. Our noble dead.

Hmmmm.

But what do the dead say?

Did anybody ever come back from the dead any single one of the millions who got killed did any one of them ever come back and say by god I'm glad I'm dead because death is always better than dishonor? Did they say I'm glad I died to make the world safe for democracy? Did they say I like death better than losing liberty? Did any of them ever say it's good to think I got my guts blown out for the honor of my country? Did any of them ever say look at me I'm dead but I died for decency and that's better than being alive? Did any of them ever say here I am I've been rotting for two years in a foreign grave but it's wonderful to die for your native land? Did any of them say hurray I died for womanhood and I'm happy see how I sing even though my mouth is choked with worms?

Nobody but the dead know whether all these things people talk about are worth dying for or not. And the dead can't talk. So the words about noble deaths and sacred blood and honor and such are all put into dead lips by grave robbers and fakes who have no right to speak for the dead. If a man says death before dishonor he is either a fool or a liar because he doesn't know what death is. He isn't able to judge. He only knows about living. He doesn't know anything about dying. If he is a fool and believes in death before dishonor let him go ahead and die. But all the little guys who are too busy to fight should be left alone. And all the guys who say death before dishonor is pure bull the important thing is life before death they should be left alone too. Because the guys who say life isn't worth living without some principle so important you're willing to die for it they are all nuts. And the guys who say you'll see there'll come a time you can't escape you're going to have to fight and die because it'll mean your very life why they are also nuts. They are talking like fools. They are saying that two and two make nothing. They are saying that a man will have to die in order to protect his life. If you agree to fight you agree to die. Now if you die to protect your life you aren't alive anyhow so how is there any sense in a thing like that? A man doesn't say I will starve myself to death to keep from starving. He doesn't say I will spend all my money in order to save my money. He doesn't say I will burn my house down in order to keep it from burning. Why then should he be willing to die for the privilege of living? There ought to be at least as much common sense about living and dying as there is about going to the grocery store and buying a loaf of bread.

And all the guys who died all the five million or seven million or ten million who went out and died to make the world safe for democracy to make the world safe for words without meaning how did they feel about it just before they died? How did they feel as they watched their blood pump out into the mud? How did they feel when the gas hit their lungs and began eating them all away? How did they feel as they lay crazed in hospitals and looked death straight in the face and saw him come and take them? If the thing they were fighting for was important enough to die for then it was also important enough for them to be thinking about it in the last minutes of their lives. That stood to reason. Life is awfully important so if you've given it away you'd ought to think with all your mind in the last moments of your life about the thing you traded it for. So did all those kids die thinking of democracy and freedom and liberty and honor and the safety of the home and the stars and stripes forever?

You're goddam right they didn't.

They died crying in their minds like little babies. They forgot the thing they were fighting for the things they were dying for. They thought about things a man can understand. They died yearning for the face of a friend. They died whimpering for the voice of a mother a father a wife a child. They died with their hearts sick for one more look at the place where they were born please god just one more look. They died moaning and sighing for life. They knew what was important. They knew that life was everything and they died with screams and sobs. They died with only one thought in their minds and that was I want to live I want to live I want to live.

He ought to know.

He was the nearest thing to a dead man on earth.

He was a dead man with a mind that could still think. He knew all the answers that the dead knew and couldn't think about. He could speak for the dead because he was one of them. He was the first of all the soldiers who had died since the beginning of time who still had a brain left to think with. Nobody could dispute with him. Nobody could prove him wrong. Because nobody knew but he.

He could tell all these high-talking murdering sonsofbitches who screamed for blood just how wrong they were. He could tell them mister there's nothing worth dying for I know because I'm dead. There's no word worth your life. I would rather work in a coal mine deep under the earth and never see sunlight and eat crusts and water and work twenty hours a day. I would rather do that than be dead. I would trade democracy for life. I would trade independence and honor and freedom and decency for life. I will give you all these things and you give me the power to walk and see and hear and breathe the air and taste my food. You take the words. Give me back my life. I'm not asking for a happy life now. I'm not asking for a decent life or an honorable life or a free life. I'm beyond that. I'm dead so I'm simply asking for life. To live. To feel. To be something that moves over the ground and isn't dead. I know what death is and all you people who talk about dying for words don't even know what life is.

There's nothing noble about dying. Not even if you die for honor. Not even if you die the greatest hero the world ever saw. Not even if you're so great your name will never be forgotten and who's that great? The most important thing is your life little guys. You're worth nothing dead except for speeches. Don't let them kid you any more. Pay no attention when they tap you on the shoulder and say come along we've got to fight for liberty or whatever their word is there's always a word.

Just say mister I'm sorry I got no time to die I'm too busy and then turn and run like hell. If they say coward why don't pay any attention because it's your job to live not to die. If they talk about dying for principles that are bigger than life you say mister you're a liar. Nothing is bigger than life. There's nothing noble in death. What's noble about lying in the ground and rotting? What's noble about never seeing the sunshine again? What's noble about having your legs and arms blown off? What's noble about being an idiot? What's noble about being blind and deaf and dumb? What's noble about being dead? Because when you're dead mister it's all over. It's the end. You're less than a dog less than a rat less than a bee or an ant less than a white maggot crawling around on a dungheap. You're dead mister and you died for nothing.

You're dead mister.

Dead.

BOOK II

The Living

Two times two is four. Four times four is sixteen. Sixteen times sixteen is two hundred and fifty-six. Two hundred and fifty-six times two hundred and fifty-six is oh well that was far enough anyhow. All right then two times three is six. Six times six is thirty-six. Thirty-six times thirty-six is five hundred and seventy-six. Five hundred and hell that wasn't any good. That was as far as he could go.

That was the trouble with numbers. They got so big you couldn't handle them and even if you could they got you nowhere. Try something else. Lie and lay. Now I lay me down to sleep. I lay these flowers on the table. I lie them on the table. I lie down to sleep. He laid there for three hours. I lie this book down. What the hell why not put it down and be done with it? Who is there? Whom is there? Of whom to who of who to whom. Between you and I and the gatepost. Between you and me. Between us that's much better. There's nobody like her. Nobody

like she. There's nobody like she is. There's nobody
like her is. Nobody like her.

David Copperfield had a tough time and was ap-
prenticed to Mr. Micawber who believed everything
would turn out well. There was an Aunt Dorrity
or something like that. David ran away to her. His
mother had big brown eyes and was gentle and Barkis
was willing. The father was dead. Old Scrooge was
tight and Tiny Tim said God bless us all. There was
a pudding round like a cannon ball with fire. Tiny
Tim was a cripple. The last of the Mohicans was an
Iroquois. Was he or wasn't he and where did Leath-
erstocking come in?

Half a league half a league half a league onward.
Into the valley of death rode the six hundred. Noble
six hundred. Theirs not to reason why theirs but to
do or die. Nothing more. When the frost is on the
pumpkin and the fodder's in the shock when you
hear the ta-de-dum-dee of the ta-da turkey cock. No
good. Maybe something else.

There are eight planets. They are Earth Venus
Jupiter Mars Mercury. One two three four five. Three
more. He didn't know. A star flickers and a planet
has steady light. He couldn't remember. Thou shalt
not have any other gods before me. Thou shalt not
kill. Thou shalt honor thy father and mother. Thou
shalt not covet thy neighbor's ox nor his ass nor his
manservant nor his maidservant. Thou shalt not
steal. Thou shalt not commit adultery. Not enough.
Blessed are the meek for they shall inherit the earth.
Blessed are the poor for they shall see god. Blessed
are they who hunger and thirst after righteousness
sake for they shall do something or other he couldn't
remember. The Lord is my shepherd I shall not

want. He leadeth me beside the green pastures. He leadeth me beside the cool waters. He anointeth my head with oil. My cup runneth over. Yea though I walk through the valley of death I shall fear no evil for thy rod and thy buckler they comfort me. Surely goodness and mercy will follow me all the days of my life and I will dwell in the house of the Lord forever. That was pretty good. That was the best yet.

Hell the trouble with him was he didn't know anything. He didn't know a thing. Why hadn't they taught him something he could remember? Why didn't he have something to think about? Here he was with nothing to do but think and he didn't have anything to fall back on. All he could remember was himself his life and that was bad. His mind was the only thing he had left and he had to find something to use it for. Only he couldn't use it because he didn't know anything. He was ignorant as a baby when he really tried to think.

If he could remember a book chapter for chapter he could lie back and read it over and over again in his mind. Only he couldn't remember. He couldn't even remember the plots much less the chapters. Only a little bit here and a little bit there. It wasn't that he had forgotten how to remember. It was just that he'd never paid any attention so he had nothing worth remembering. He was a man he was alive he would be alive for a long time and he had to have something to do something to think about. He had to start in like a baby and learn. He had to concentrate. He had to start in at the beginning. He had to start in with an idea.

The idea had been seeping into his mind for a

long while just how long he didn't know and the idea was this that the important thing is time. He remembered from ancient history in the tenth grade that way way back even before Christ the first men who began to think were thinking of time. They studied the stars and figured out the week and the month and the year so that there would be some way of measuring time. That was smart of them because he was about in the same fix they were and he knew that time was the most important thing in the world. It was the only real thing. It was everything.

If you can keep track of time you can get a hold on yourself and keep yourself in the world but if you lose it why then you are lost too. The last thing that ties in with other people is gone and you are all alone. He remembered how the Count of Monte Cristo when he was put into his dungeon down there in the darkness kept a record of time. He remembered how Robinson Crusoe was very careful to keep track of time even though he never had any appointments. No matter how far you are separated from other people if you have an idea of time why then you are in the same world with them you are part of them but if you lose time the others go on ahead of you and you are left alone hanging in air lost to everything forever.

All he knew was that on a day in September in 1918 time stopped. There was a howl somewhere and he dived into a dugout and things blotted out and he lost time. From that instant to the present he might as well figure that there was a chunk of time he could never regain. Even if he discovered a way to check up on time from now on that which was gone was lost forever and he would always be living behind the rest of the world because of it. He could remember nothing after the explosion until he woke up and realized he was deaf. His wounds were very serious and he might have been unconscious for two weeks two months six months before he awakened who could tell? And then afterwards the faintings in and out and the long periods when he simply lay in between thinking and dreaming and imagining things.

When you're completely unconscious there is no such thing as time it goes like the snap of your finger you're awake and zip you're awake again with no idea of how long a time passed between. Then when you're fainting in and out time must still seem shorter than to a normal person because you're really half crazy and half awake and time bunches up on you. They said his mother was in labor three days when she had him and yet when it was all over she figured she had been in labor for about ten hours. Even with pain and everything time had seemed shorter to her than it really was. Now if all this was true he probably had lost more time than he suspected. He might even have lost a year two years. The idea gave him a funny prickling feeling. It was a kind of fear yet not like any ordinary fear. It was more of a panic it was the panicky dread of losing yourself even from yourself. It made him a little sick at his stomach.

The whole idea had been taking form in his head for a long while the idea of trapping time and getting himself back into the world but he hadn't been able to concentrate on it. He had drifted off into dreams or he had found himself suddenly in the middle of thinking of something entirely different. Once he thought he had the problem solved by the visits of the nurse. He didn't know how many times she came into his room every twenty-four hours but she must have a schedule. All he had to do was to count the seconds then the minutes then the hours between each visit she made until he had twenty-four hours counted and after that he would be able to figure the days simply by counting her visits. There would be no danger of a slip-up because the vibration of her footsteps always awakened him. Then just in case the spacing of her visits might be changed sometime he could figure out things like the number of his bowel movements each day and he could also figure out the other things which happened maybe only two or three or four times a week like his baths and the changing of his bed clothes and mask. Then if any of these things changed he could check up on it by the others.

It took a long time to make his mind stick on the idea long enough to figure out this formula because he wasn't used to thinking but in the end he thought it through and started putting it into effect. The instant the nurse left him he began to count. He counted to sixty which meant a minute as nearly as he would ever be able to figure it. Then in one side of his mind he checked up the minute he had measured and began counting from one to sixty again. The first time he tried it he got up to eleven minutes before his mind slipped off the track and his figures were lost. It happened like this. He was counting along on the seconds when all of a sudden he thought maybe you're counting too fast and then he thought remember it seems to take a sprinter an awful long time to run a hundred yards yet he does it in only ten seconds. Then he slowed down his counting while he watched an imaginary sprinter step off a hundred yards and then he was in the middle of a high school track meet Shale City against Montrose watching Ted Smith run the hundred yard dash and win it with his head high lunging for the tape and all the kids from Shale City yelling their heads off and then he had lost count.

That meant he had to wait all over again for the nurse because she was his starting point. It seemed like hundreds maybe thousands of times that he got started out and then lost track and had to sink back angrily into the darkness of his mind and wait for the vibration of her feet and the feel of her hands on him again so he could start anew. Once he got up to a hundred and fourteen minutes and thought I wonder how long a hundred and fourteen minutes is in hours and stopped in spite of himself to figure it out and discovered it was an hour and fifty-four minutes and then he remembered a phrase fifty-four forty or fight and almost went crazy trying to recall where it came from and what it meant. He couldn't remember and when he got back to the counting he realized that he had lost a lot of minutes in thinking and so even though he had broken a record he was no farther along than when the idea of time first entered his mind.

On that day he realized he was tackling the thing from the wrong angle because to figure it out he would have to stay for twenty-four hours in a stretch counting steadily all the time without making a mistake. In the first place it was almost impossible for a normal person to stay awake counting that

long much less a guy whose body was two-thirds
asleep to begin with. And in the second place he
couldn't help making a mistake because he couldn't
keep the minute figures separate in his mind from
the second figures. He would be counting along on
the seconds when all of a sudden he would get
panicky and think how many minutes was it I had?
And even though he was almost positive it was
twenty-two or thirty-seven or whatever it was the
tinge of doubt that had first caused him to ask the
question hung on and then he was sure he was
wrong and by that time he had lost count again.

He never succeeded in counting the time from
one visit to the next but he began to realize that
even if he did he would then have to keep three sets
of figures the seconds the minutes and the count of
the nurse's visits until twenty-four hours were com-
pleted. Then he would have to stop sometime to
reduce the minutes to hours because when the minute figures got too high he wouldn't be able to remember them at all. So with the hours he would
have a fourth set of figures. In counting just the
seconds and minutes which was as far as he ever
got he tried to pretend that they were actual figures
that he could see on a blackboard. He pretended he
was in a room with a blackboard on the right side
and another on the left. He would keep the minutes
on the left hand blackboard and then they would be
there when he needed to add another to them. But
it didn't work. He couldn't remember. Each time he
failed he could feel choking gasps in his chest and
stomach and he knew that he was crying.

He decided to forget all about the counting and
to check up on simpler things. It didn't take long to

discover that he had a bowel movement about once in every three visits from the nurse although sometimes it took four visits. But that didn't tell him anything. He remembered that doctors used to say twice a day was healthy but the people doctors were talking about had normal food and they ate it with their mouths and swallowed it with their throats. The stuff he was fed might give him a much higher average than ordinary people. Then again just lying in his bed from one year to the next he might not need much food and so his score might be much less than ordinary people. He also discovered that his bath and change of bed clothes came about once in every twelve visits. It was thirteen once and another time only ten so he couldn't count on it absolutely but it was at least a figure. He was a little surprised to discover that where he had first thought of seconds and minutes he was now thinking of days and even series of days. That was how he got on the right track.

It came to him while he was lying and feeling with the skin of his neck the line that the covers made at his throat. He got to imagining them a mountain range snuggling down against his throat. He had one or two strangling dreams from them but he kept on thinking. He got to thinking that the only part of him that wasn't covered up that was free that was just as it should be was the skin on the sides of his neck which went from the cover-line to his ears and the half of his forehead above the mask. That skin and his hair. He says to himself maybe there is some way you could use those patches of skin they are free to the air and they are healthy and a guy with as few healthy things as you've got should put them to use. So he got to thinking of what a man did with skin and he realized that it was used to feel with. But that didn't seem enough. He thought about skin some more and then he remembered that you could also sweat with it and that when you started sweating you were hot but by the time the sweat covered your skin you were cool from the air drying the sweat. That was how he got the idea of heat and cold and that was how he came to wait for the sunrise.

The whole thing was so simple that his stomach grew hard with excitement just from thinking about it. All he had to do was to feel with his skin. When the temperature changed from cool to warm he would know it was sunrise and the beginning of a day. Then he would check right through counting the nurse's visits to the next sunrise and then he would have the number of her visits per day and he would forever afterward be able to tell time.

He started trying to stay awake until the change in temperature occurred but half a dozen times running he fell asleep before it happened. Other times he got confused thinking to himself is it hot now or is it cool what kind of a change am I waiting for maybe I am running a fever maybe I am too excited and am sweating from excitement and that would spoil the whole thing oh please god don't let me sweat don't let me run a temperature let me know whether I'm hot now or whether I'm cold. Give me some idea of when the sunrise is coming and then I'll be able to catch it. And then after a long long while with a lot of false starts he said to himself here sit down and think this thing over seriously. Right now you're panicky you're too anxious and

132

you're blundering. Each time you make a mistake you've lost more time and that is one thing you can't afford to lose. Think what usually happens in the morning in a hospital and try to figure out what follows that. That's easy he said to himself in the mornings in a hospital nurses try to get their heavy work done. That meant that he was bathed and his bed clothes were probably changed in the morning. He would have to take that as his starting point. He would have to assume a few things and the first assumption would be that this was true. He already knew that the bath and change of bedding came on an average of once in every twelve visits.

Now he had to begin assuming again. You would think in a hospital like this that your bedding would be changed at least every other day. Maybe it was once a day but he didn't think so because at the rate of one change in every twelve visits that would make the nurse visit him every two hours and there was so little to do he couldn't see why her trips should be that often. So he would figure that every two days she bathed him and changed his bed clothes and that she did this in the morning. If this was true then she came into his room six times in a day and night. That would make it every four hours. The simplest schedule for her to follow would be to come in at eight twelve four eight twelve four and so on. She would probably change the bedding as early as possible in the morning so that would be at eight o'clock.

Now he said to himself what is it you want to try to check up on the sunrise first or the sunset? He decided it was the sunrise because when the sun sets the warmth of the day usually hangs on and the

133

change is so slow that those two pieces of skin on his neck might not be able to catch it. But in the early dawn everything is cool and almost the first flash of sunlight should give some kind of heat. At least the change should be more complete in the morning than at night so he would catch the sunrise.

He had a panicky minute when he thought what if you are on the west side of the hospital and the setting sun comes in full on the bed and then you'll mistake that for sunrise? What if you're on the north or south side of the hospital and never get the direct sunlight at all? Maybe that would be simpler. Then he realized that even if he were on the west side and caught the heat of the setting sun he would still have the visits of the nurse to check on to tell him which was which because by now he was convinced she changed the bed clothes in the morning.

Now you damn fool he said to himself you're getting things so complicated you'll never come out if you don't stop. The first thing to do is to catch the sunrise. Next time the nurse comes into the room and bathes you and changes the bed clothes you are going to assume it is eight o'clock in the morning. Then you can think about anything you want to without worrying or you can even go to sleep because each time she comes in she awakens you. You will wait and count five more visits and that should make the fifth one somewhere around four o'clock in the morning. Four o'clock in the morning is just before sunrise so after the fifth visit from the nurse you will stay awake and concentrate every bit of your mind and skin on the job of catching the temperature change when it comes. Maybe it'll work and maybe it won't. If it does all you have to do is to wait six more trips and see if there is another sunrise and if there is you'll have the number of trips every twenty-four hours and that will give you a way of setting up a calendar around the nurse's visits. The important thing is to catch two sunrises in a row and then you have trapped time forever then you can begin to catch up with the world.

It was eight visits later before he felt the nurse's hands on him as she took off his nightshirt and began to sponge his stump with warm water. He felt his heart quicken and his blood send a warm glow of excitement to his skin because he was going to start out once more to trap time only now he was doing it smartly he was doing it wisely. He felt himself rolled over on his side and held there while the bed quivered from the nurse's work. Then he was rolled back between crisp cool sheets. The nurse thumped around at the foot of the bed for a minute. He felt the vibrations of her footsteps as she walked from place to place in the room. Then the vibrations receded and there was a sharp little tremor of the door closing and he knew he was alone.

Calm down he said to himself calm down because you haven't proved anything yet. You may have this thing doped out all wrong. Maybe the things you've assumed are all wrong. If they are then you've got to make a whole new set of assumptions so don't get so cocky. Just calm down and lie back and count five more visits. He dozed a little and he thought of a lot of things but always on the blackboard in his mind he kept the number two or three or whatever it was and finally the fifth visit came with the nurse's feet vibrating against the floor and her hands on him and on the bed. According to the things he had figured out it should now be four o'clock in the morning and in a little while depending on whether it was winter or summer or fall or spring the sun would rise.

When she left he began concentrating. He didn't dare fall asleep. He didn't dare permit his mind to wander for one minute. He didn't dare let the suffocating excitement that was all over him and inside of him interfere with his thinking and feeling as he lay there waiting for the sunrise. He had come on the trail of something so precious and so exciting that it was almost like being born all over again into the world. He lay there and thought in one hour three hours certainly in ten hours I will feel a change on my skin and then I will know whether it is day or night.

It seemed that time was standing perfectly still just to spite him. He got panicky little spasms when he felt sure the change had occurred without him catching it and with each little spasm he seemed to get sick to his stomach. Then there would be a clear period when he would very calmly feel with his skin and convince himself that he was sane that he hadn't fallen asleep and missed it that his mind hadn't wandered that the change was still ahead.

And then all of a sudden he realized it was coming. The muscles in his back and thighs and stomach stiffened because he knew it was coming. He could almost feel the sweat squeeze out of his body as he tried to hold his breath lest he miss it. The pieces of skin on each side of his neck and the half of his forehead seemed to tingle as if they had been paralyzed and now were getting a fresh supply of blood.

136

It felt as if the pores of his neck were actually reaching out to grab at the change to suck it in.

The whole thing was so slow so gradual that it seemed impossible it was happening at all. There was no danger now of his mind wandering or of falling asleep. It would be like falling asleep in the middle of a first kiss. It would be like falling asleep in the middle of running a hundred yard dash and winning it. The only thing he could do was wait and feel out with his skin and catch every second of the change every slow movement of time and temperature as they offered him a return of life.

It seemed like he lay there stiff and expectant and excited for hours. There were times when he was sure that the nerves of his neck were not registering when it seemed they had suddenly gone numb and that the change might slip away from him. And then there were other times when it felt as if his nerves had jabbed through so near the surface of his skin that there was actual pain sharp and fine and penetrating as they groped to register the change.

And then the thing began to happen swiftly and more swiftly and although he knew he was in a sheltered hospital room as far removed as possible from changes in temperature it seemed to him when it came that it came in a blaze of heat. It felt like his neck was seared burned scorched from the heat of the rising sun. It had penetrated his room. He had recaptured time—he had won his fight. The muscles of his body relaxed. In his mind in his heart in whatever parts of him that were left he was singing singing singing.

It was dawn.

All over the world or at least all over the country

137

to which he had been brought the sun was rising in the east and people were getting out of bed and the hills were turning pink and birds were singing. All over Europe or all over America it was sun-up. What the hell did it matter if you didn't have any nose so long as you could smell the dawn? He lay without nostrils and he sniffed. He caught the smell of dew on grass and he shivered because it was so delicious. He shaded his eyes against the first bright rays of the morning sun and looked off and he saw the high mountains of Colorado in the east and he saw the sun coming over them and he saw colors creeping down their sides and in the nearer distance he saw rolling brown hills which became pink and lavender like the inside of a seashell. And still closer in the field in which he stood and clear up to his ankles he saw the green grass and it was sparkling and he burst into tears. He thanked god that he could see the dawn.

He turned from the sunrise and looked toward the little town in which he lived toward the little town in which he had been born. All of the rooftops were rosy with the dawn. Even the houses that were unpainted and square and squat and ugly were beautiful. He heard the lowing of cows waiting to be milked in back yards for the town in which he had been born was a very sensible town and each man had his cow. He heard the slam of back screen doors as sleepy householders went to the chicken yard or to the barn yard to take care of their animals. And he could see inside the houses where men were getting out of bed and yawning healthily and scratching their chests and groping for house slippers and finally get-

138

ting up and going into the kitchen where their wives had sausages and hot cakes and coffee for them.

He saw babies squirming in their cribs and rubbing their eyes with tiny fists and maybe smiling or maybe crying and maybe smelling a little bad but looking awfully healthy as they greeted the sunshine as they greeted the morning as they greeted the dawn. He saw all of these things all of these beautiful homely things as he looked toward the town and he had only to turn from the town to look at the sun and the mountains.

Oh god god thank god he thought I've got it now and they can't take it away from me. He thought I have seen the dawn again and I will see it every morning from now on. He thought thank you god thank you thank you. He thought if I never have anything else I will always have dawn and morning sunlight.

New year's eve. Snow flying in the air wet snow
clouds sifting close over Shale City. Everything still
with lights glowing inside warm houses. No confetti
no champagne bottles no yelling no noise at all. The
quietude of new year for ordinary people who
worked and were kind and wanted only peace. Happy new year. His father kissing his mother and saying happy new year my dear we've been lucky the
kids are healthy I love you happy new year I hope
the new one turns out as well as the old.

New year's eve at the bakery with guys saying
goddam I'm glad it's over the next one can't be any
worse happy new year hell let's go out into the fog
and get drunk. Walking out of the bakery on new
year's eve with the bins every which-way and the
ovens empty and the conveyors stopped and the
wrapping machines paralyzed and the dividers still
and nobody but the crew going out of a strange
silent place with their voices echoing flatly against

dead machinery. The guys at the bakery going out to celebrate the new year.

The guys in saloons shoving free ones across the bar and saying happy new year and many more of them kid you been a good customer have one on the house happy new year and the hell with the prohibitionists some day the bastards are going to give us trouble. The girls from the hash houses and the girls from the hotels and the guys swarming out of dirty little apartment bedrooms and music and dancing and smoke and somebody with a ukulele and have another and the feeling of being lonesome that everybody has inside him and people bouncing against you and off you and have another one and a girl passing out at the bar and a fight and happy new year.

Oh god the happy happy new year he had counted three hundred and sixty-five days and now it was new year's eve.

It didn't seem like a year. It had gone by like a lifetime when you look back and think of a time so far away that you can't clearly remember what happened yet a time that has gone so quickly it seems only a minute ago it started. Six visits from the nurse each day—thirty days to a month—and now three hundred and sixty-five days. It had gone quickly because he was doing something he was keeping track of time like other people he had sets of figures to remember he controlled a little world of his own lagging behind that on the outside but still nearer to it than before. He had a calendar in which the sun and the moon and the seasons had no place a calendar with thirty days for each month and twelve months in the year and now five extra days to make up the difference with the nurse's next visit to make it new year's morning.

He had been a very busy guy and he had learned a lot. He had learned how to check everything against something else so that he couldn't possibly lose the grip he had gained on time. He could tell day from night without straining for the sunrise. He knew exactly what visit from the nurse would bring him a bath and a change of bed clothes. When the schedule was interrupted and the nurse was a visit late he grew disappointed and sullen and tried to imagine what she was doing but when she finally came he was always excited.

He could even tell his nurses apart. The day nurse was steady but the night nurses seemed to change. The day nurse had smooth slick hands a little hard like the hands of a woman who has worked a long while so he guessed that she was middle aged and he imagined her with gray hair. She always came directly to the bed from the door in four firm steps so he figured that his bed was about ten feet from the door. Her footsteps were heavier than the night nurses' so he took her for a large woman. Her steps were almost as heavy as those of the doctor who came in once in a great while and poked around for a little time and then went away. The day nurse had a brisk way of doing things—flip and he was on his side whoosh and a sheet slid next to him flop and he was on his back swipe-swipe and he was bathed. She knew her business this old day nurse and he liked her. Once in a great while she came in at night instead of the night nurse. He always squirmed to let her know he was pleased to see her and she patted him on the stomach and ran her hand through the thin hair on his skull to tell him thanks and how are you?

The night nurses were irregular. Sometimes he would have two or three of them the same week. Most of them took more steps from the door to the bed than the day nurse and their treads were lighter. They closed the door softer or harder and they wandered around the room more. Mostly their hands were very soft and just moist enough to go bumpily instead of smoothly over his body. He knew they were young. When a new nurse came in he always knew what she would do first. She would pull the covers off him and then she would make no movements for a minute or two and he would know she was looking at him and probably getting a little sick. One of them turned and ran out of the room and didn't come back. That way he didn't get his urinal and so he wet the bed but he forgave her for it. Another one cried. He felt her tears on the chest of his night shirt. He got a little passionate because he suddenly felt she was very close to him and he lay in pain for hours after she left. He imagined her young and beautiful.

All of these things were interesting they were important they kept him a very busy guy. He had made a new universe he had organized it to his liking and he was living in it. And this was new year's eve although on the outside it might be the Fourth of July for all he cared. He named the days of the week Monday through Sunday and he named the months so he could celebrate the holidays. Each Sunday afternoon he went for a walk in some woods that were just outside Paris. Once in springtime when he was on leave he walked in them so now it was springtime every Sunday afternoon as he walked through the woods in his uniform with his chest way out and his legs pumping and his arms swinging free. When July came and the trout were biting he went up to Grand Mesa and talked things over with his father. They had lots to talk about they had learned lots since the last time they saw each other. It's much better than worrying his father said you worry so much you don't enjoy life death is better only I wish I knew how your mother was.

Each night summer and winter week in and week out he went to sleep with Kareen whispering to her god bless you Kareen darling god bless you. I don't know what I'd do without you here beside me every night the others have all gone and I'm alone except for you Kareen. They slept with his arm around her or her's around him and they always turned together. They nestled tight against one another and he kissed her in his dreams all night long.

A year—what a hell of a long time a year was. Kareen was nineteen that day a minute ago when he said goodbye to her at the railroad station. He was four months in training camp and eleven months in France so that made her over twenty. Then the time he had lost completely would probably even it up to another year. And now another. And others to come others and others. Kareen must be twenty-two by now. She was at least twenty-two. Three years. It would go on that way as long as he lived. Ten more years and Kareen would have lines. A little later and her hair would be gray and then she would be an old woman an old old woman and the girl at the station would never have existed.

He knew it wasn't true. Kareen would never grow

144

old. She was still nineteen. She would be nineteen forever. Her hair would stay brown and her eyes clear and her skin fresh like rain. He would never let one line mark her face. That was something he could do for her that no other man on earth could ever do. He could keep her safe beside him young and beautiful forever safe from time in the world he had built where time moved according to orders and every Sunday was spring. But where would she be— the real Kareen—the Kareen out in the world out in time? While he slept with the nineteen year old Kareen every night was the real Kareen with somebody else a woman now perhaps with a baby? Kareen grown up and far away having forgotten him . . .

He wished he could be near her. Not that he could ever see her not that he wanted her to see him. But he would like to feel that he was breathing the same air she breathed that he was in the same country she was in. He remembered the funny excitement inside him when he used to start out for old Mike's house for Kareen's house. The closer he got the sweeter the air seemed. He used to tell himself although he knew it wasn't true that the air around her house was different because it was near to her.

He had never cared particularly where he was where they had taken him—but thinking now of Kareen he got homesick. His mind was wailing I wish to god I was in America I wish I was home. It seemed that an American any American was a friend compared to any Englishman or Frenchman. That was because he was an American himself America was his home he had been born there and anyone outside was a stranger. Then he would say to himself what do you care you'll never be able to see or talk or walk you won't know the difference you might as well be in Turkey as America. But that wasn't true. A guy liked to think he was home. Even though he could do nothing but lie in blackness it would be better if the blackness were the blackness of home and if the people who moved in the blackness were his own people his own American people.

But that was too much to hope for. In the first place a blast strong enough to tear his arms and legs off must have blown all identification to hell and gone. When you have only a back and a stomach and half a head you probably look as much like a Frenchman or a German or an Englishman as an American. The only way they would have of telling what country he was from would be by the place they found him. And he was pretty sure he had been found among Englishmen. The regiment had been stationed right alongside a Limey regiment and when they went over the top both the Americans and the Limeys went together. He remembered very clearly that the Americans shifted to the left among the Limeys because there was a little hill just in front of the American position. The Germans on the hill had all been wiped out two days before so there was no use of the Americans puffing their way up it. They all shifted to the left as they went over and they were all mixed up with the Limeys. He remembered looking around when he dived into that dugout and seeing only two Americans and all the rest Limeys. Just a flash of them just a thought of them then blackness.

So he was probably in some crummy English hospital with people all taking him for a Limey and on the report sent home about him there was nothing except missing in action. Maybe it was just as well he was eating through a tube that English coffee was so stinking bad. Roast beef and pudding and soggy pastries and bad coffee. It was just as well. Only he wasn't any American any longer he was an Englishman. He was a Limey and probably a citizen at that. It gave him a lonesome feeling just to think about it. He'd never had any particular ideas about America. He'd never been very patriotic. It was something you took without even thinking. But now it seemed to him that if he were really lying in an English hospital he had lost something he could never hope to get back. For the first time in his whole life he felt that it would be a little pleasant a little comforting to be in the hands of his own people.

Those Limeys were a funny bunch of guys. They were more like foreigners than the Frenchmen. A Frenchman you could understand but a Limey was always twitching his nose and you couldn't understand him at all. When you were stationed right next to them for two months you began to understand just how foreign they were. They did some funny things. There was a little Scotchman in the Limey regiment who threw down his gun and quit the war when he heard that the Huns on the other side of Nomansland were Bavarians. The little Scotchman said that the Bavarians were commanded by Crown Prince Rupert and that the Crown Prince was the last Stuart heir to the throne of England and the rightful king and that he would be goddamed if he would fight his king just because some Hanoverian pretender told him to.

Now in any ordinary army they would take you out and shoot you for a thing like that. But that's the way Limeys were funny. This little guy caused a hell of a stink. Two or three of his officers argued with him very politely instead of shooting him and when they couldn't get him to see things their way they called the colonel. So the colonel came and had a long talk with the Scotchman and everybody seemed puzzled and the Scotchman got tougher and tougher and dared them to shoot him because he said his court martial would bring out the truth that everything was a fraud and King George would have to resign and how would Lloyd George like that? The colonel went away and the Scotchman stayed sitting down on the bottom of the trench and pretty soon there came an order from G.H.Q. transferring him back of the lines for six weeks or until the Bavarians went away so he wouldn't have to fire in the direction of troops commanded by his king. That was how funny Limeys were and that was how both the Americans and the Limeys knew there were Bavarians across from them.

Then take Lazarus. He showed up one gray morning when nothing was happening. All of a sudden out of the fog loomed this big fat Hun coming toward the British lines. Afterwards there was a lot of talk about what he was doing there all alone in the first place. Probably he was on patrol duty and had lost his way or else he was trying to desert or maybe he had gone a little crazy and was just wandering around out there among the barbed wire and the shell holes for the hell of it. He had a kind of aimless way of pitching from side to side. He would hit a line of barbed wire and stumble and try to feel his way along it for a minute. Finally he would climb it awkwardly like a drunk and come jerking on toward the Limeys.

It was a pretty dull morning and the Limeys were cold and uncomfortable and sore about the war so somebody took a shot at the Hun. The poor guy stood stock still peering through the fog like he was surprised anybody would want to shoot him. Then the whole Limey regiment began to pop off at him. Even as his body sagged he had a kind of hurt and puzzled look. They let him lie out there with one arm hung over the barbed wire like a sentry who was pointing the way for someone else.

Nobody paid any attention to him for several days and then both the Americans and the Limeys began to notice that when the wind was right that Hun was raising quite a stink. But it was only when the wind was just so and nobody cared much until one day when the colonel who had sent the little Scotchman back of the lines came through on inspection. The colonel was a great guy to stand on form. Corporal Timlon who came from Manchester always swore that in a pinch the colonel would execute nine men to keep up the morale of the tenth. Anyhow the colonel was walking along with his moustache waxed and his bony old nose high in the wind when all of a sudden he got a sniff of the Hun.

That's a very strong odor he said to Corporal Timlon. He's a Bavarian sir said Corporal Timlon they always smell worse. The colonel coughed and blew his nose and said very bad for the morale of the men very bad take a squad out tonight and bury him corporal. Corporal Timlon started to explain that things were pretty fidgity out there even at night but the colonel interrupted him. And corporal he said stuffing his handkerchief back into his pocket don't forget—a word of prayer. Corporal Timlon said yes sir and then looked hard at his men to see who was grinning so that he could figure who to take out on the burial squad.

So that night Corporal Timlon took a detail of eight men. They dug a hole and pushed that Bavarian into it and the corporal said a word of prayer like the colonel told him and they filled the hole and came on back. The air was pretty well cleaned up next day but the day after that Heinie got a little nervous and began dropping shells all around the Limey regiment. The Limeys weren't hurt any but one of the big ones happened to catch the Bavarian. He leaped into the air like in a slow motion picture and landed high and dry on the wire again with his finger pointing toward the Limey regiment exactly like a stool pigeon. That was when Corporal Timlon started calling him Lazarus.

Things were pretty busy that day and all through the night. Every time the Limeys had an idle half hour they would shoot at Lazarus in kind of a lazy way hoping they might knock him off the wire because they knew the nearer he was to the ground the less he would smell and that Bavarian was getting awfully gamy. But he managed to hang onto the wire and the next morning the colonel came through again. First thing he did was sniff the air and get a strong flavor of Lazarus. He turned to Corporal Timlon and said Corporal Timlon when I was subaltern an order was an order and not just an interesting suggestion. Yes sir said Corporal Timlon. You will take a full burial squad out tonight said the

colonel and you will bury the corpse six feet deep.
And just so that you will not take orders so lightly
in the future you will read the full service of the
Church of England over the body of our fallen
enemy. But sir said Corporal Timlon you see things
have been pretty heavy here and——

That night Corporal Timlon took a full burial
squad out. They also took a sheet to wrap Lazarus
in. It wasn't very tasty work because Lazarus had
gotten to the runny stage by that time but they
wrapped him in the sheet and planted him six feet
deep and then all of them stood around the grave
while Corporal Timlon read the burial service maybe skipping over a few ands and ors but getting the
general idea across pretty well.

About the middle of the service a couple flares
went up from the other side and just as the corporal
was throwing the third handful of dirt into Lazarus'
face somebody got a bead on him and shot him
right smack through the bottom. Corporal Timlon
hollered out god 'ave mercy on your soul amen
those bloody barstards 'ave shot me in the arse that's
wot they've done mike for cover men. And they all
scrambled back to the lines.

Corporal Timlon got eight weeks hospital leave
which was lucky for him because the whole Limey
regiment was almost wiped out three weeks later. A
couple days after Corporal Timlon was shot Lazarus
stopped another one and hit the fence again with his
sheets flapping in the wind and parts of him dripping
toward the ground. One of the Limeys said that was
to be expected because Bavarians never held up
very well after the first week. The whole regiment
opened fire on poor Lazarus and managed to shoot

him off the wire. You could still smell him but you couldn't see him any more so everybody tried to forget him. They would have too if it hadn't been for the new subaltern.

He was just a kid only eighteen with wavy blonde hair and blue eyes looking like a six foot baby anxious as hell to win the war all by himself. He was a cousin of the captain or something and the officers made a regular pet out of him. He came up to the front two days after Lazarus was shot off the wire. The Limeys were so fond of him they kept him pretty well under cover and the kid somehow got the idea he was being picked on and that the men would think he was a coward. He begged all the time to be assigned to night patrol duty and when it was no go he sneaked out on his own one night. They missed him about three o'clock in the morning and it was almost dawn before they found him. Somehow he had wandered out beyond the first line of barbed wire. When they came on him he was lying on his stomach in a pool of vomit. In stumbling through the barbed wire he had fallen and struck his right arm clean up to the shoulder through Lazarus.

The detail that found him brought him to the officers' dugout. He was babbling and crying and smelling to high heaven. The captain sent him back the same night. He said it was a penalty for befouling the officers' dugout and he got very stern when anyone inquired what had happened to the kid. When Corporal Timlon came back with his seat repaired and someone told him the story he asked well how is the kid getting along? A little guy named Johnston who kept the whole regiment posted on such things said oh hell he's mad as a hatter they haven't even

152.

let him out of the straightjacket yet. Well said Corporal Timlon when is he going to get better? The doctors say he ain't never going to get better said Johnston he's bad off that one.

Poor young blonde English guy wanting to win the war so bad and going stark crazy before he even got into action. Poor Limey kid somewhere in a hospital behind barred windows yelling and crying and brooding forever. That was a funny thing. The young Limey had legs and arms and he could talk and see and hear. Only he didn't know it he couldn't get any fun out of it there was no meaning to it for him. And lying in another English hospital was a guy who wasn't a bit crazy but who wished he was. He and the young Limey should swap minds. Then they'd both be happy.

Somewhere crying and sobbing in the dark—it was night now almost new year's—there was the young Limey. And here he was in the dark sobbing and crying too. On new year's eve. Poor young Limey don't cry it's just new year's just think a whole fresh year stretching out in front of both of us. Wherever you are Limey—and maybe you're right here in this same hospital—wherever you are we have lots in common we are brothers young Limey happy new year to you. Happy happy new year. . . .

During the second year of his new time world nothing happened except that once a night nurse stumbled and fell to the floor setting up a fine vibration in his bedsprings. During the third year he was moved to a new room. The heat of the sun in the new room came in over the foot of his bed and by checking against the bath hour he figured that his head was to the east and his other end to the west. His new bed had a softer mattress and its springs were stiffer. They carried vibrations longer and that helped him a great deal. It took him months to locate the door and the dresser but they were months filled with calculation and excitement and finally with triumph. They were the shortest months he could remember in his whole life. All of this made the third year whisk by like a dream.

The fourth year started very slowly. He spent a lot of time trying to remember the books of the bible in their order but the only ones he could be sure of were Matthew Mark Luke and John and First and Second Samuel and First and Second Kings. He tried to put words to the story of David and Goliath and Nebuchadnezzar and Shadrack Meshack and Abednego. He remembered how his father used to yawn loudly around ten o'clock at night and stretch his arms and get up out of his chair and say Shadrack Meshack and to bed we go. But he couldn't remember the stories that went with the characters very clearly so they were poor time fillers. That was bad because when he couldn't fill in the time he got to worrying. He got to thinking I wonder if I haven't made a mistake in figuring the days the weeks the months? He got to thinking it wouldn't be impossible to drop even a whole year if a person were careless. Then he would get excited and frantic. He would check back and back to make sure he hadn't made a mistake so far back that he would get more confused than before. Every time he fell asleep he tried to have the day and month and year numbers firmly planted in his mind lest he forget them while he dreamed and every time he awakened his first panicky thought leaped at the terrible possibility he might not have remembered correctly the numbers he had in his mind when he fell asleep.

And then an astonishing thing happened. One day toward the middle of the year the nurse gave him a completely fresh change of bed linen when he had received a change only the day before. This had never happened before. Every third day he was changed no sooner and no later. Yet here everything was upset and for two days in a row he was getting the change. He felt all in a hub-bub. He felt like bustling around from room to room and chattering about how busy he was and what great things were going to happen. He felt all bright with expectation and excitement. He wondered if he would get a fresh change of linen every day from now on or whether they would return again to the old schedule. This was as important as if an ordinary man with legs and arms and other parts were suddenly confronted with the possibility of living in a new house every day. It would be something to look forward to from day to day throughout the years. It would be something to break up time to make it something a guy could stand without mulling over Matthew Mark Luke and John.

Then he noticed something else. In addition to giving him an unexpected bath the nurse was spraying him with something. He could feel the spray cool and misty against his skin. Then she put a clean nightshirt on him and folded the covers back at his throat. This was different too. He could feel her hand through the covers as it passed over the fold smoothing smoothing smoothing. He was given a fresh mask which the nurse arranged very fussily so that it fell to his throat and there was carefully tucked under the fold of the bedcovers. After that she combed his hair carefully and left. He could feel the vibrations of her footsteps as she went away and the little jar of the door closing behind her. Then he was alone.

He lay perfectly still because it was a very luxurious feeling to be so completely redone. His body glowed and his sheets were cool and crisp and even his scalp felt good. He was afraid to move for fear he would spoil the good feeling. There was only a

moment of this and then he felt the vibrations of
four maybe five people coming into his room. He
lay tense trying to catch their vibrations and wondering why they were there. The vibrations got heavier
and then they stopped and he knew that people were
gathered around his bed more people than ever before had been in his room at the same time. It was
like the first time he went to school and was embarrassed and bewildered with so many people
around. Little tremors of expectations ran through
his stomach. He was stiff with excitement. He had
visitors.

The first thought that passed through his mind
was that they might be his mother and sisters and
Kareen. There was just a chance that Kareen forever lovely and young was standing by him was
looking down at him was even this minute putting
out her hand her soft and tiny hand her beautiful
beautiful hand to touch his forehead.

And then just as he could almost feel the touch of
her hand his delight turned suddenly to shame. He
hoped more than anything else in the world that it
was not his mother and sisters and Kareen who had
come to visit him. He didn't want them to see him.
He didn't want anybody he had ever known to see
him. He knew now how foolish it had been to
wish for them as sometimes in his loneliness he had.
It was all right to think about having them near it
was comforting it was warm and pleasant. But the
idea that they might be beside his bed right now was
too terrible to cope with. He jerked his head con-
vulsively away from his visitors. He knew this dis-
lodged his mask but he was beyond thinking of
masks. He only wanted to hide his face to turn his

blind sockets away from them to keep them from
seeing the chewed up hole that used to be a nose
and mouth that used to be a living human face. He
got so frantic that he began to thrash from side to
side like someone very sick with a high fever who
can only monotonously repeat a motion or a word.
He fell into his old rocking motion throwing his
weight from one shoulder to the other back and
forth back and forth back and forth.

A hand came to rest on his forehead. He quieted
because it was the hand of a man heavy and warm.
Part of it lay on the skin of his forehead and part of
it he felt through the mask which cut across his
forehead. He lay still again. Then another hand began to fold the covers back from his throat. One
fold. One and a half folds. He grew very quiet very
alert very curious. He thought very hard about who
they might be.

Then he had it. They were doctors come to ex-
amine him. They were visiting firemen. He was probably a very famous guy by this time and the doctors
were beginning to make pilgrimages. One doctor was
probably saying to the others you see how we were
able to do it? You see what a clever job we did?
You see where the arm came off and you see the
hole in his face and you see he still lives? Listen to
his heart it's beating just like your heart or mine. Oh
we did a fine job when we got him. It was a great
piece of luck and we're all very proud. Stop by in
my office on your way out and I'll give you one of
his teeth for a souvenir. They take a wonderful
polish he was young you see and his teeth were in
good condition. Would you like a front one or would

you prefer a good thick tusker from farther back? The thick ones look best on a watch chain.

Somebody was plucking at his nightshirt over his left breast. It was as if a forefinger and thumb were pinching up a portion of it. He lay very quiet now deathly quiet his mind jumping in a hundred different directions at once. He could sense that something important was about to happen. There was a little more fumbling with the pinch of nightshirt and then the cloth fell back against his chest once more. It was heavy now weighted down by something. He felt the sudden coolness of metal through his nightshirt against his chest over his heart. They had pinned something on him.

Suddenly he did a curious thing he hadn't done for months. He started to reach with his right hand for the heavy thing they had pinned on him and it seemed that he almost clutched it in his fingers before he realized that he had no arm to reach with and no fingers for clutching.

Someone was kissing his temple. There was a slight tickling of hair as the kiss was given. He was being kissed by a man with a moustache. First his left temple and then his right one. Then he knew what they had done to him. They had come into his room and they had decorated him with a medal. He knew furthermore that he must be in France instead of England because French generals were the ones who always kissed you when they handed out medals. Still that might not be true. American generals and English generals shook your hand but since he had no hand to shake maybe this was an Englishman or an American who had decided to follow the French custom because there was no other way to do it. But still the chances now seemed even that he was in France.

When he snapped back from thinking of where he was and adjusting himself to the idea that it might be France he was a little surprised to find that he was getting mad. They had given him a medal. Three or four big guys famous guys who still had arms and legs and who could see and talk and smell and taste had come into his room and they had pinned a medal on him. They could afford to couldn't they the dirty bastards? That was all they ever had time to do just run around putting medals on guys and feeling important and smug about it. How many generals got killed in the war? There was Kitchener of course but that was an accident. How many others? Name them name any of the soft-living sons-ofbitches and you could have them. How many of them had got all shot up so they had to live wrapped in a sheet for the rest of their lives? They had a lot of guts coming around and giving medals.

When he had thought for an instant that his mother and his sisters and Kareen might be standing beside the bed he had wanted to hide. But now that he had generals and big guys he felt a sudden fierce surging desire for them to see him. Just as before he had started to reach for the medal without an arm to reach with so now he began to blow the mask off his face without having mouth and lips to blow with. He wanted them to get just one look at that hole in his head. He wanted them to get their fill of a face that began and ended with a forehead. He lay there blowing and then he realized that the air from his lungs was all escaping through his tube. He began to

roll again from shoulder to shoulder hoping to dislodge the mask.

While he lay there rolling and puffing he felt a
vibration way down in his throat a vibration that
might be a voice. It was a short deep vibration and
he knew that it was making a sound to their ears.
Not a very big sound not a very intelligent sound
but it must seem to them at least as interesting as
the grunting of a pig. And if he could grunt like a
pig why then he was accomplishing a great thing because before he had been completely silent. So he
lay thrashing and puffing and grunting like a pig
hoping that they would see damned well how much
he appreciated their medal. While he was in the
middle of this there was an indefinite churning of
footsteps and then the departing vibrations of his
guests. A moment later he was all alone in the blackness in the silence. He was all alone with his medal.

Suddenly he quieted. He was thinking about the
vibrations of those footsteps. He had always carefully felt for vibrations. He had measured the size of
his nurses and the dimensions of his room by them.
But suddenly to feel the vibrations of four or five
people tramping across the room made him think. It
made him realize that vibrations were very important. He had thought of them up to this time only
as vibrations coming to him. Now he began to consider that also there could be vibrations going from
him. The vibrations which he received told him
everything—height weight distance time. Why
shouldn't he be able to tell something to the outside
world by vibrations also?

In the back of his mind something began to glimmer. If he could in some way make use of vibrations

he could communicate with these people. Then the glimmer became a great dazzling white light. It opened up such breathless prospects that he thought he might suffocate from sheer excitement. Vibrations were a very important part of communication. The fall of a foot on the floor is one kind of vibration. The tap of a telegraph key is simply another kind.

When he was a kid way back maybe four years ago or five he had a wireless set. He and Bill Harper used to telegraph each other. Dot dash dot dash dot. Particularly on rainy nights when their folks wouldn't let them go out and there was nothing to do and they just lounged around the house and got in everybody's way. On such nights he and Bill Harper used to dot and dash at each other and they had a hell of a good time. He still remembered the Morse code. All he had to do in order to break through to people in the outside world was to lie in bed and dot dash to the nurse. Then he could talk. Then he would have smashed through his silence and blackness and helplessness. Then the stump of a man without lips would talk. He had captured time and he had tried to figure geography and now he would do the greatest thing of them all he would talk. He would give messages and receive messages and he would have made another step forward in his struggle to get back to people in his terrible lonely eagerness for the feel of people near him for the things that were in their minds for the thoughts they might give him his own thoughts were so puny so unfinished so incomplete. He would talk.

Tentatively he raised his head from the pillow and let it fall back again. Then he did it twice quickly.

That would be a dash and two dots. The letter d. He tapped out SOS against his pillow. Dot-dot-dot dot dot dot-dot-dot. SOS. Help. If there was anybody in the whole world needed help he was the guy and now he was asking for it. He wished the nurse would hurry back. He began to tap out questions. What time is it? What's the date? Where am I? Is the sun shining or is it cloudy? Does anybody know who I am? Do my folks know I'm lying here? Don't tell them. Don't let them know anything about it. SOS. Help.

The door of the room jarred open and the nurse's footsteps came up to the bed. He began to tap out more frantically now. Here he was right on the brink of finding people of finding the world of finding a big part of life itself. Tap tap tap. He was waiting for her tap tap tap in response. A tap against his forehead or his chest. Even if she didn't know the code she could tap just to let him know she understood what he was doing. Then she could rush away for someone who could help her get what he was saying. SOS. SOS. SOS. Help.

He felt the nurse standing there looking down at him trying to figure out what he was doing. The mere possibility that she didn't understand after all he had gone through before discovering it himself shocked him into such excitement and fear that he began to grunt again. He lay grunting and tapping grunting and tapping until the muscles in the back of his neck ached until his head ached until he felt that his chest would burst from his eagerness to shout out to explain to her what he was trying to do. And still he felt her standing motionless beside his bed looking down and wondering.

Then he felt her hand against his forehead. For just a moment she held it there. He kept on tapping growing angry now and hopeless and feeling like he wanted to throw up. She began to stroke his forehead in slow gentle motions. She was stroking it in a way she had never done it before. He felt pity in the softness of her touch. Then her hand went from his forehead clear back through his hair and he remembered that Kareen used to do that sometimes. But he put Kareen out of his mind and kept right on tapping because this was such an important thing that he couldn't stop for pleasant sensations.

The pressure of the hand against his forehead was getting heavier. He realized that she was trying by the weight of her hand to make him tired so he'd quit tapping. He began to tap all the harder all the faster to show her that her plan wouldn't work. He could feel the vertebrae in the back of his neck crack and pop from the strain of this unexpected work. The nurse's hand grew heavier and heavier on his head. His neck grew tireder and tireder. It had been a terrible day a long day an exciting day. His tapping grew slower and her hand got still heavier and finally he lay back very quietly against the pillow while she brushed his forehead.

He had lost all track of time. All his work to trap it all his counting and calculation of it might just as well never have happened. He had lost track of everything except the tapping. The instant he awakened he began to tap and he continued until the moment when drowsiness overcame him. Even as he fell asleep the past portion of his energy and thought went into the tapping so that it seemed he dreamed of tapping. Because he tapped while he was awake and dreamed of tapping while he was asleep his old difficulty in distinguishing between wakefulness and sleep sprang up again. He was never quite positive that he was not dreaming when awake and tapping when asleep. He had lost time so utterly that he had no idea how long the tapping had been going on. Maybe only weeks maybe a month perhaps even a year. The one sense that remained to him out of the original five had been completely hypnotized by the tapping and as for thinking he

165

didn't even pretend to any more. He didn't speculate about the new night nurses in their comings and goings. He didn't listen for vibrations against the floor. He didn't think of the past and he didn't consider the future. He only lay and tapped his message over and over again to people on the outside who didn't understand.

The day nurse tried hard to soothe him but she did it only as if she were trying to calm an irritable patient. She did it in such a way that he knew he would never break through as long as he had her. It never seemed to occur to her that there was a mind of intelligence working behind the rhythm of his head against the pillow. She was simply watching over an incurably sick patient trying to make his sickness as comfortable as possible. She never thought that to be dumb was a sickness and that he had found the cure for it that he was trying to tell her he was well he was not dumb any longer he was a man who could talk. She gave him hot baths. She shifted the position of his bed. She adjusted the pillow in back of his head now higher now lower. When she moved it higher the increased angle bent his head forward. After tapping for a time in this position he could feel pain shooting all the way down his spine and across his back. But he kept right on tapping.

She got to massaging him and he liked that she had such a brisk gentle touch to her fingers but he kept on tapping. And then one day he felt a change in the touch of her fingers. They were not gentle and brisk any longer. He felt the change through the tips of her fingers through the tenderness of her touch he felt pity and hesitancy and a great gathering love that was neither him for her nor her for him but rather a kind of love that took in all living things and tried to make them a little more comfortable a little less unhappy a little more nearly like others of their kind.

He felt the change through the tips of her fingers and a sharp little twinge of disgust went through him but in spite of the disgust he was responding to the touch responding to the mercy in her heart that caused her to touch him so. Her hands sought out the far parts of his body. They inflamed his nerves with a kind of false passion that fled in little tremors along the surface of his skin. Even while he was thinking oh my god it's come to this here is the reason she thinks I'm tapping goddam her god bless her what shall I do?—even while he was thinking it he fell in with her rhythm he strained to her touch his heart pounded to a faster tempo and he forgot everything in the world except the motion and the sudden pumping of his blood . . .

There was a girl named Ruby and she for him was the first. It was when he was in the eighth maybe the ninth grade. Ruby lived down in Teller Addition on the other side of the tracks. Ruby was younger than he maybe only in the sixth or seventh grade but she was a great big girl an Italian and very fat. All the boys in town somehow began with Ruby because she never embarrassed them. She came right to the point and that was that although once in a while you had to tell her she was pretty. But no other nonsense and if a guy didn't have any experience why Ruby never laughed at him and never told on him she just went right ahead and gave it to him.

The guys liked to talk about Ruby when there wasn't anything better to talk about. They liked to laugh about her in such talks and say oh no I never see Ruby any more I manage to get around I'm finding something new every day. But that was all talk because they were really very young guys and Ruby was the first and only girl they knew they were too shy with other girls with nice girls. They soon grew ashamed of Ruby and when they went down they would always feel a little dirty and a little disgusted. They came away blaming Ruby somehow for making them feel that way. By the time they got to the tenth grade none of them would ever speak to Ruby and finally she disappeared. She just wasn't around any more and they were all kind of glad they didn't have to meet her on the street.

There was Laurette down at Stumpy Telsa's place. Stumpy Telsa had a house in Shale City. She had five or six girls there and the finest pair of Boston bulls in town. The guys when they were young when they were maybe fourteen or fifteen used to wonder a great deal about Stumpy Telsa's place. For them it was the most wonderful the most exciting the most mysterious house in Shale City. They would hear stories from older guys on what went on down there. They could never quite decide whether they were for it or against it but they were always interested.

One night three of them went down through the alley in back of Stumpy Telsa's and crept through the back yard and tried to peek in through the kitchen door. There was a colored cook there making sandwiches and she saw them and let out a howl. Stumpy Telsa came swinging into the kitchen on her peg leg and grabbed a butcher knife and came out into the back yard. They all ran like hell with Stumpy Telsa yelling after them that she knew who they were and she was going right inside and phone their folks. But it was a bluff. Stumpy hadn't seen their faces and she didn't telephone anybody.

Later on when they were seventeen or eighteen and practically ready to get out of high school he and Bill Harper decided the hell with talking about the place all the time so they went down to Stumpy Telsa's one night to find out for themselves. They walked right into the front room and nobody pulled a knife on them or anything. It was about eight o'clock and evidently things weren't busy because Stumpy came into the parlor and talked to them and wasn't sore at all. They were too embarrassed to say anything to Stumpy about why they came and Stumpy didn't say anything to them about it either so it turned out to be just a visit. Stumpy called upstairs to the girls for a couple of them to come down and sit in the parlor and she told the colored woman to make up a plate of sandwiches. Then she went away. Alone in the parlor they could hear the two girls coming down from upstairs and they knew that now they were going to find out whether all the things they had heard about such places were true. Some guys said that the girls came right smack into the parlor stark naked and other guys said they'd never let you see them naked they always wore a kimono or something. Nothing they hated said these guys so much as a man who wanted to see them without any clothes at all. So they sat with their hearts in their throats and waited and watched.

But when the girls came down they were fully

dressed. They were dressed better than most of the
girls in Shale City and they were prettier than most
of them too. They came in and sat down and they
talked just like anybody else would talk. One of
them seemed to like Bill Harper the best and the
other one seemed to like him. The one who liked him
talked about books all the time. Had he read this
had he read that and he hadn't read any of them
and he got to feeling pretty much like a dummy.
After about a half hour of munching sandwiches and
talking about books Stumpy Telsa came in all beam-
ing and smiling and told them it was time to go
home. So they got up and shook hands with the two
girls and went away.

That night they took a long walk through the
town discussing all the things they had heard about
Stumpy Telsa's place and deciding they were either
lies or else they were the kind of guys that women
didn't like in that way. That was bad maybe they'd
be failures with women all their lives maybe there
was something they didn't have. They decided not
to tell anybody about their visit because they felt
they were much more disgraced than if things had
turned out differently.

Later on he got to thinking about the girl who
talked books and after thinking about it for a long
while he went down to see her again. Her name was
Laurette and she seemed glad to see him. She told
him if he wanted to see her always to be sure he
made it before nine o'clock because after that time
things were generally pretty busy. He did come
again and several times more and always they sat
in the parlor and always they talked. He got to
thinking maybe I'm in love with Laurette now

wouldn't that be a fine thing me falling in love with
her and how would I break the news to my mother
and father? And on the other hand he would think
why is it that all we do is talk what does she think
I am? All during the winter of that year and on
through the spring he went down to see Laurette
once maybe twice sometimes even three times a
month. And each time he went down just before he
knocked on the door he would pull himself together
and he would say to himself Joe Bonham be a man
this time. But Laurette was so nice he couldn't
figure out how a fellow started things like that without seeming kind of dirty. So he never did.

When he graduated from high school he got a pair
of gold cuff links through the mail and all they had
with them was a card that had the initial L written
on it. He had a hell of a time explaining to his folks
who sent him the links but he prized them very
highly and he decided that tomorrow night after grad-
uation he would go down to Stumpy Telsa's. Now
that Laurette had told him in a kind of roundabout
way that she loved him things would be different. So
about nine o'clock on the big night he went down to
Stumpy Telsa's still hunting for some pleasant and
polite way to express the thing that was in his mind.
He knocked on the door and Stumpy Telsa invited
him in and when he asked for Laurette she told him
Laurette wasn't there. Where had she gone? She had
gone to Estes Park. Every year said Stumpy Telsa
she takes three months off up there. All winter long
she buys new clothes and she saves her money and
for three months she lives at the best hotel in Estes
Park. She goes out with guys and she dances and
she dearly loves to have the guys fall in love with

171

her and when they fall for her she is always nice to them but she is never too nice. She is never as nice as they want her to be. She is a smart girl that Laurette said Stumpy Telsa she eats her cake and she has it too. And on top of that she saves her money and she has a nice little bankroll. Why don't you get a job in some other town and then come around in the fall after Laurette is rested up and talk things over with her? Maybe you and Laurette would be very happy. But by the time fall came he was working in a bakery fifteen hundred miles away and he never saw Laurette again.

There was a girl named Bonnie. She clapped him on the back one day while he was sitting in Louie's drug store near the bakery having a coke. She slapped him on the back and she said to him you're Joe Bonham ain't you Joe Bonham from Shale City? Well I'm Bonnie Flannigan we used to go to school together Jesus it's good to see somebody from god's country. He looked at her and he couldn't remember her at all. Oh yes he said I remember you. She nodded and said you were ahead of me in school and you never would give me a tumble how are you and why don't you come over to see me sometime? I live in the bungalow court just three doors from the bakery. You work in the bakery I know. I see some of the guys once in a while sweet guys all of them they told me you were there.

He looked at her and he could tell she was younger than him and he could tell what she was. He felt a little pain in his stomach because girls like that might come from New York or Chicago or St. Louis or Cincinnati they might come from Denver or Salt

Lake or Boise Idaho or Seattle but they never came from Shale City because Shale City was home.

He went over to see her. She wasn't a small girl and she wasn't a very cute girl but she was awfully good natured and she was busy with plans for the future and she was full of life. I been married three times already said Bonnie I been married three times and all my husbands said I looked just like Evelyn Nesbitt Thaw. Do you think I look like Evelyn Nesbitt Thaw?

In the mornings around five or six o'clock sometimes they would go over to Main Street for breakfast over in the bright cheap shiny white tiled restaurants where you could get anything for a dime. They would go there and the place would be filled with sleepy sailors wondering what to do now that it was morning and Bonnie would know them all. She would slap them on the shoulders as they walked toward their booth and she would call them by name. Hi Pete well if it ain't old Slimy hi Dick well if it ain't old George. When they got to the booth and ordered their ham and eggs she would say to him Joe if you're a smart guy you'll stick with me. You want to go through school huh? Joe you stick with me. I'll send you through school. I make the fleet and I know all these guys and I know where their pocketbooks are and I'm smart and careful I never even had clap you stick with me Joe and we'll wear diamonds. See that guy over there? He always says I look just like Evelyn Nesbitt Thaw do you think I look like Evelyn Nesbitt Thaw dearie?

There was a girl named Lucky. She was the Statue of Liberty and Aunt Jemima and the girl-you-left-behind to about a half a million doughboys in

Paris. They had a regular American house in Paris
and when they were on leave there when they were
away from the trenches and the killing all the guys
went to the American house and talked to American
girls and drank American whiskey and were happy.

Lucky was the best one of the bunch the nicest
and about the smartest. She would receive him in her
room and she would be stark naked with a great red
scar where somebody had yanked her appendix. He
would come into her room pretty tired at the end of
a night and maybe a little drunk and he would lie
down on her bed and put his hands behind his head
and watch Lucky. The minute she saw him she would
smile and go over to her dresser and out of the top
drawer she would bring a doily. She was always
crocheting on that doily. She would sit at the foot
of the bed all brightness and gossip and friendliness
and crochet the doily and talk to him.

Lucky had a son. He was six maybe seven years
old and Lucky was keeping him in a school on Long
Island. She was going to raise him to be a polo
player because polo players got around and they met
all the best people and nothing was too good for
Lucky's son he was such a cute little bastard. Figuring out the house percentage and towel expenses and
medical care Lucky still made herself from a hundred
fifty to two hundred dollars a week at two dollars
apiece. But of course we live it up we got to dress
up to our positions it costs lots in clothes I can tell
you but a girl's got to look smart.

Lucky had been in the San Francisco earthquake.
She must have been sixteen or seventeen then and
that would make her almost thirty now. When the
earthquake hit San Francisco Lucky was on the

fourth floor of a hotel on Market Street. I was entertaining a gentleman friend and when I first felt that thing hit I said to myself Lucky I said that's an earthquake and you ain't going to be caught dead with no son-of-a-bitch on top of you. So I pushed him off and I run right down into the street stark naked and you should of seen the guys stare.

To talk with Lucky to be with Lucky to lie with Lucky was like finding peace in a heathen country it was like breathing the air of a place you love when you're sick and dying for a breath of it. To see her smile to hear her bright chatter to watch her bony little fingers fly as they worked the crochet needle with the night noises of Paris a foreign city just outside the window was enough to make anybody feel better and less lonely.

Paris was a strange city a foreign city a dying city a lively city. It had too much life and too much death and too many ghosts and behind the bars of the cafes too many dead soldiers. Have a drink. Oh Paris is a woman's town with flowers in her hair. No doubt about it Paris was a wonderful town a woman's town but it was also a man's town. Ten thousand doughboys tommies poilus on leave ten thousand a hundred thousand of them. A few days boys a few days and then you go back and each time you go back the chances are more against you than they were the last time. Remember that there is a law of averages so come on dearie turn a trick five francs ten francs two dollars oh boy what's that an American voice? me for her. What the hell a song in the parlor and a swig of cheap cognac and let's go because out there in the east the place they call the western front there is a little old guy keeps a book

and figures averages all day long and all night long
he never makes a mistake. Flor da lee. Flor da lee.
God save the king. Come on up honeybunch lonesome wanta try something new parley vous fransays?
A gallon of red wine like water and sourdough bread
and maybe please god I find an American girl who
don't talk heathen languages. Jig-jig hell that's not
what I want. I want something loud because there
is a voice I want to drown out. It's a voice that
doesn't make any sound but I can't get away from
it.

*Somewhere it is being prepared. Somewhere deep
in the heart of Germany the shell is being made.
Some German girl is polishing it right now polishing
it and cleaning it and fitting the charge into it. It
glistens in the factory light and it has a number and
the number is mine. I have a date with the shell. We
shall meet soon.*

Motor lorries rumbling through the street gathering guys up outside gathering up the late ones saying come on buddy time's up down to the station
and jump on the old box car. Because you're going
back. Back to the little old guy who figures out there
the guy who figures all day long and all night long
and never makes a mistake. The stars and stripes
forever ta-da da-de-um and da-de-ah. Try it kid it's
good some guys say it's got dope in it don't believe a
thing they tell you. Some guys say it dries you out.
It's called absinthe let it filter down in your glass it's
swell. Parley vous parley vous yes sir no sir lonesome honey where's that American voice? god I'd
like to find her. Where's Jack where's Bill where's

John gone all gone. Gone west. Taps. Ten thousand dollars for the folks back home. Ten thousand simoleons Jesus. I know a house on Rue Blondel black and white all nations. Americans? Sure anything you want oh god that isn't what I want what I want's a long way off but I'll take whatever you got. It's a long way to Tipperary. Lights out.

Nearer nearer. Some top-heavy canvas-covered German truck is plunging toward France right now. In it are shells and among the shells the one with my number. It's coming toward the west through the Rhine valley I always wanted to see it through the Black Forest I always wanted to see it through the deep deep night coming toward France the shell I shall meet. It's coming nearer and nearer nothing can stop it not even the hand of god for I have a time set and it has a time set and we shall meet when the time comes.

America expects every man to do his duty France expects every man to do his duty England expects every man to do his duty every doughboy and tommy and poilu and what the hell did they call the Italians? anyhow they're expected to do their duty too. Lafayette we come and so in Flanders fields the poppies blow between the crosses row on row check off the rows for the little old guy with the book the little old guy who figures all day long and all night long and never makes a mistake. Oui oui parley vous jig-jig? Sure jig-jig what the hell five francs ten francs who says two dollars two good old American dollars and a glass of corn whiskey? My god this cognac I always thought it was a swell drink I heard

177

so much about it it's terrible give me corn and what do you think of the prohibitionists? Four million of us gone four million votes I suppose we don't count they'll ruin us yet let's go out and hunt corn good old American corn. Darling honey deary sweet tired lonesome wanta friend take a table take a chair take a bed only don't take too long there's lots of guys Paris is full of them so don't take too long.

Hidden beneath some gentle rolling hill that is like a woman's breast on the solid flesh of the land hidden under the hill in some unknown ammunition dump is my shell. It is ready. Hurry boy hurry doughboy don't be late finish whatever you have to do you haven't much time left.

Sing a rag-time jig-jig sing a rag-time mam'selle sing a hot time in the old town tonight. Sing a Joan of Arc and a flor da lee sing a mademoiselle from Armentieres. Sing a Lafayette parley vous fransays. Get up and jump jump mighty fast make the smoke whirl in the air smash the chairs smash the windows tear down the house goddam it move boy move girl put cognac in your joints and turn the lights out and beat the drums and get out of the trenches by christmas and see Paris by night and turn a trick for five francs and oui-oui parley vous hunky-dory corn in my belly and a little old guy with a book who figures all day long and all night long and he figures faster and faster faster and quicker harder and stronger and faster faster faster.

It will come with a rush and a roar and a shudder. It will come howling and laughing and shrieking and

*moaning. It will come so fast you can't help yourself
you will stretch out your arms to embrace it. You
will feel it before it comes and you will tense yourself for acceptance and the earth which is your
eternal bed will tremble at the moment of your
union.*

Silence.

What's this what's this oh my god can a man ever
get lower can a man ever be less?

Weariness and gasping convulsive exhaustion. All
life dead all life wasted and becoming nothing less
than nothing only the germ of nothing. A kind of
sickness that comes from shame. A weakness like
dying weakness and faintness and a prayer. God
give me rest take me away hide me let me die oh
god how weary how much already dead how much
gone and going oh god hide me and give me peace.

XV

He kept on tapping

He kept on now for another reason aside from the simple desire to speak which had started him out. He kept on tapping because he didn't dare stop he didn't dare think. He didn't have the courage to ask himself even so simple a question as how long will it be before the nurse understands what I am doing? Because he knew it might be months it might be years it might be all the rest of his life. All the rest of his life to be tapping when the merest whisper—one word with the syllables barely formed by two lips—when that was all he needed to tell what he wanted.

There were times when he knew he was stark raving crazy only from the outside he realized he must seem as he always had seemed. Anyone looking down at him would have no way of suspecting that beneath the mask and the mucus there lay insanity as naked and cruel and desperate as insanity could ever be. He understood insanity he knew all about it now. He understood the overpowering impulse to kill without having a reason for killing the desire to beat against living skulls until they were pulp the passion to strangle the lust for murder that was more beautiful more satisfying more imperative than any lust he had known before. But he couldn't do it he couldn't kill he couldn't do anything but tap.

Inside his skull there was a normal man with arms and legs and everything that goes with them. It was he Joe Bonham trapped in the darkness of his own skull rushing frantically from ear-hole to ear-hole wherever in the skull there might be an opening. Like a wild animal he was trying to hammer his way out to escape into the world beyond. He was trapped in his own brain tangled in the tissues and brain-matter kicking and gouging and screaming to get out. And the only person in the world who could help him had no idea of what he was doing.

He got to thinking this nurse is keeping me a prisoner. She is keeping me more securely a prisoner than any jailer than any chain than any stone wall they could ever build around me. He got to thinking of all the prisoners he had ever read about or heard about all the little guys from the beginning of the doing of things who had been caught and imprisoned and who had died without ever becoming free again. He thought of the slaves little guys like himself who had been captured in war who had spent the rest of their lives chained like animals to oars rowing some big guy's ship through the Mediterranean sea. He thought of them down there in the deeps of the ship never knowing where they were going never smelling the outer air never feeling anything except the oar in their hands and the shackles on their legs and the whip that lashed their backs when they grew tired. He thought of them all the shepherds and farmers and clerks and little shopkeepers who had suddenly been taken away from their way of living who had been cast into the ships and had stayed there away from their homes and their families and their native parts until finally they collapsed at their oars and died and were thrown out into the sea for the first time to touch fresh air and clean water. He thought of them and he thought they were luckier than I am they could move they could see each other they were more nearly living than I and they were not imprisoned as securely.

He thought of the slaves deep under the street levels of Carthage before the Romans came and destroyed the city. He remembered from some time way back in the past how he had read of the Carthaginian slaves and what they did and how they were treated. How the great Carthaginian lords wanting someone to guard their treasure stores would find a healthy young man and put out his eyes with sharp sticks so he wouldn't be able to see where they took him and thus learn the location of their treasures. Then they would take him poor blinded young guy down into the passages under the level of the streets to the door of the treasure house. There they chained one arm and one leg to the door and one arm and one leg to the wall so that for anyone to enter the seal would have to be broken and the seal was the living breathing body of a man. He thought of the Carthaginian slaves down in the darkness blinded and chained and he thought they were lucky guys. They died soon there was no one there to take care

182

of them to make sure the breath of life stayed in their bodies as long as possible. They were in agony but they died soon and even in their agony they could stand on two legs they could pull against their chains. They could hear and when someone spoke some great noble coming down into the treasure house they could hear the blessed sound of a human voice.

He thought of the slaves who built the pyramids thousands of them tens of thousands of them spending their whole lives to put up a dead monument to a dead king. He thought of the slaves who fought each other in the Coliseum in Rome for the entertainment of big guys who sat in the boxes and held their thumbs up or down to give the slaves life or death. He thought of the slaves when they disobeyed —ears lopped off hands hacked away screaming tongues flexed with cries for mercy even as they were pulled out by the roots so that no secrets would be betrayed. Little guys all over the world shot drowned stabbed crucified boiled in oil whipped to death burned at the stake—all these things were the fate of slaves the fate of the little guy the fate of men like himself. Only the slaves could always die but he couldn't and he was mutilated far beyond any slave who ever lived. Yet he was one of them he was part of them he too was a slave. He too had been taken away from his home. He too had been put into the service of another without his consent. He too had been sent to a foreign country far from his native parts. He too had been forced to fight against other slaves of his own kind in a strange place. He too had been mutilated and branded forever. He too was at last a prisoner in the narrowest

183

cell of them all the cell of his own horrible body awaiting only the relief of death.

God help us he thought god help us all the slaves. For hundreds and thousands of years we have been tapping we slaves tapping away from the depths of our prisons. All of us all of the little guys all the slaves from the beginning of time tapping tapping tapping——

A man had come into the room a man with heavy footsteps. The man came over to the bed and threw the covers back and began to prod his body. It was the doctor. He could imagine the nurse going for the doctor and saying that thing up there in the room that thing is always tapping its head. I get nervous I think it needs something. Come and look at it come and try to stop its tapping. So the doctor had come and now he was prodding him. When the prodding was over the doctor took the tube from his throat and he had a little fit of strangling like he always had when they took the tube out to clean it. The doctor put the tube back in its hole and stood quietly doing nothing.

All during this he kept up his tapping and now that the doctor was quiet he tapped much harder. It was just possible that the doctor might understand what he was trying to do. He felt the vibration of the doctor's footsteps moving over toward the dresser then coming back again. He felt a cold wet thing against the stump of his left arm. Then he felt a sharp little sting a sharp little pain like a needle and he knew the doctor was injecting something into his arm.

Before he began to feel its effects he knew it was some kind of dope. They were trying to shut him up.

They had been trying all along they knew perfectly
well what he was doing nobody with any brains could
fail to know. And he knew what they were doing too.
They were plotting against him out there in the darkness. They had tried every way on earth to make him
be still but he had out-fought them he had kept
right on tapping. So now they were doping him. They
were forcing him to be silent. They didn't want to
hear him. They weren't interested in anything but
getting him off their minds. He shook his head frantically to try to tell them that he didn't want to be
doped. Then the needle was withdrawn and he knew
it didn't matter whether he wanted it or not.

He determined to keep on with his tapping in
spite of them to try to strengthen his will to such a
point that even as the drug overcame him even as he
fell completely asleep from its effects the strength of
his will would carry over into his sleep and he would
continue the tapping just as you turn on a machine
and it continues to operate after you have gone away.

But a fog settled down over his mind a numbness
took possession of his flesh so that it seemed that
each time he lifted his head from the pillow he was
lifting some enormous weight. The weight grew
heavier the tapping grew slower his flesh became
like the flesh of a dead person his mind seemed to
shrink and shrivel as the drowsiness swept over it.
In his last moment of thinking he was saying to
himself they've won again but they can't win forever
they can't forever oh no not forever . . .

xvi

Things began slowly to change to go in wide hazy circles to dissolve into one another. It seemed that he was relaxing in every muscle of his body relaxing in his brain. The bed felt softer than it had ever been before. The pillow at the back of his head was like a pillow of cloud. The covers across his stomach and chest were covers of silk of cobweb of soft warm air. There was nothing below him nor above him nor to his right nor to his left. His skin went limp and lazy against his flesh and even his blood seemed at rest not pumping through his heart any more but lying warm and liquid and still in his veins.

And yet in the midst of this enormous quiet there was movement. This perfectly still thing which was him his body and his mind was moving slowly through a windless world. Only it wasn't the world. It was simply space a kind of glowing space through which he was moving whether slowly or rapidly he couldn't tell because there was no air to stir at his passing. It was the kind of motion a star must make a star without atmosphere or life as it completes its steady circle through nothingness.

And there were colors everywhere. Not rough nor violent colors but the kind of shadings the sky takes on at sunrise the pinks and blues and lavenders of the inside of a seashell suddenly grown bigger than the sky and everything in it. The colors floated toward him floated into him dissolved through the particles of his body and then passed on to make way for more colors more and more and more so wonderful so beautiful so big. There were cool colors sweet smelling colors colors that made faint high music as they passed through him. He could hear the music everywhere and yet it wasn't loud. It was a kind of music that seemed to be so thin it was scarcely sound at all. It was simply a part of space a sound that was the same thing as space and color a sound that was nothing at all and at the same time more real than flesh and blood and steel. The music was so sweet so tinkling high that it seemed a part of him just as much a part as the little fibres of his body. The music was like a white ghost in the daytime. He and space and the colors and the music were the same thing. His body had drifted into them like smoke into the sky and now he like them was a portion of time.

Then the music stopped and there was silence. It wasn't the simple silence that sometimes comes when you are in the world the silence which is merely the absence of noise. It wasn't even the silence that comes to deaf people. It was something like the silence you hear when you put a seashell to your ear the silence of time itself that is so great it makes a noise. It was a silence like thunder in the distance. It was silence so dense that it ceased to be silence. It changed from a thing to a thought and in the end it was only fear.

He hung there in the silence waiting for the thing to happen. He didn't know what the thing would be but he knew it would happen. It was as if he had already seen the puff of smoke from a dynamite charge and now was waiting for the sound. Then the silence was shattered by his fall. His breath was forced back into his lungs from the pressure of the air through which he fell. He was falling a million times faster than a shooting star falling faster than light travels falling through ten thousand years and ten thousand worlds with things becoming louder and faster and more terrible. Great round globes bigger than the sun bigger than the whole milky way came at him so fast they might have been cards shuffled through a pack. They came at him and hit him full in the face and burst like soap bubbles to make way for the next and the next. His brain was working so fast that he had time to flinch for each one and after it had burst to prepare himself for the shock of the next.

He began to whirl faster than the propeller of an airplane and the whirling made noises in his head. He heard voices all the voices in the world voices that had arms and legs voices that reached out to grab him and voices that kicked as he sped by. Things went so fast before his eyes that he could see nothing but light. When he saw the light he knew that nothing was real because real things make shadows and shut out light.

And then all sound seemed centered in one voice that filled the whole world. He listened to the voice because it had stopped his fall. It had become everything—the world and the universe and the nothingness around them. It was a woman's voice crying and he had heard it before.

Where's my boy where's my boy? He's under age can't you see? He just came up from Tucson about a week ago. They had him in jail for a tramp and I came all the way here to get him back. They let him out of jail if he'd join the army. He's only sixteen except he's big and strong for his age he always was. He's too young I tell you he's just a baby. Where is he my little boy? He just came up from Tucson you see and I came to take him home.

The voice faded away but he knew the whole thing now. That boy was Christ. There wasn't any doubt about it. The boy was Christ and he had come up from Tucson and now his mother was hunting and crying for him. He could see Christ coming up from Tucson trembling out of the desert heat waves with purple robes flowing from him like in a mirage. Christ came right into the railway station and sat down with them.

It seemed like there must be a little room somewhere off from the station and they were playing blackjack there waiting for the train to go. He didn't know the other guys and they didn't know him but it didn't seem to make any difference. Outside the crowds were yelling and the bands were playing and here he was with four or five guys in a quiet little room and they were playing blackjack when Christ came up from Tucson and walked in on them. The guy with red hair looked up and said you play blackjack? and Christ said sure and the guy who looked like a Swede said then pull up a chair. Table stakes said the guy with red hair and be sure your bet's out before the first card. Christ said okay and fished around in his pocket and pulled out a quarter and laid it down.

The guy with red hair began to deal and everybody began to watch the cards except the Swede who grunted and said Christ I wish we had a drink here. Christ kind of grinned and said why don't you drink it if you want it so bad? The guy who looked like a Swede turned and looked at Christ and then he looked down at the table and sure enough there was a glass of whiskey sitting by his right hand and everybody had a drink of whiskey sitting there. They all looked up at Christ and the guy with red hair said how in hell did you do that? Christ just smiled and said I can do anything hit me only not too hard. The dealer hit him and Christ looked at the card like it was bad news. Then he pushed his money toward the dealer. I never could hit a twelve he said in a complaining voice. I don't understand it because a twelve shouldn't be any harder to hit than a thirteen should it? It shouldn't be only it is said the guy with red hair. There is nothing to that it's all the bunk said the guy who looked like a Swede a twelve is just like any other number above it only better and anybody tells you any different is filled with superstition. Gosh said a quiet little guy who had been winning and now was sampling the whiskey this stuff is mighty good liquor try it. It ought to be good said Christ still looking at his dough out there on the table it's sixteen years old.

All of a sudden the guy with red hair threw down his cards and stood up stretching and yawning. Well he said it's all aboard outside I got to go. We all got to go. I'm going to be killed on the twenty-seventh of June and I got to say goodbye to my wife and kid. The kid he's only a year eight months but smart as hell already I'd like to see him when he's five. I can see myself getting killed plain. It's just after daybreak all cool and nice with a brand new sun and the air smelling good. We're going over and I'm a sergeant by then so I go over first. Just as I get my head over the edge a bullet hits me like a hammer. I fall back clear across the trench and try to tell the other guys to go on without me only I can't talk and they go over anyhow. I lie there seeing only their legs as they run by and climb up and disappear. I kick and squirm for a minute like a chicken and then I snuggle down against the dirt. That bullet got me in the throat so I just snuggle down there peaceful like and watch the blood run out and then I'm dead. But my wife don't know it so I got to tell her goodbye just like I thought I was coming back.

Hell said the little guy who had been winning you talk like you was the only one. We're all going to be killed that's why we're here. Christ he's already dead and the big Swede over there is going to catch flu and die in camp and you in the corner you're going to get blown so damned high nobody'll ever have a souvenir and me I'm going to get buried in a trench cave-in and smother now isn't that a hell of a way to die?

All of a sudden they were all quiet listening and the guy with red hair said what's that? Somewhere in the air way far above them there was music. It was high thin music like a ghost passing through the sunlight. It was pale white music so beautiful so very faint and yet loud enough for all of them to hear. It was music like a soft breeze that finds its way out beyond the place where there is air where there is only space. It was music so faint so shivery so sweet that it made them all tremble as they stood and listened. It is the music of death said Christ the high thin music of death.

Everybody was still for a minute and then the little guy who had been winning said what the hell's this other guy doing here he ain't going to die. And then everybody looked at him. For a minute he didn't know what to say he felt like somebody who's come to a party he hasn't any invitation to and then he cleared his throat and said maybe you're right but I'm going to be the same as dead. You see I'm going to have my arms and legs blown off and my face shot out so I can't see or hear or talk or breathe and I'm going to live even if I am dead.

They all looked at him and finally the guy who looked like a Swede said Jesus he's worse off than we are. There was a little more silence and all of them seemed to be looking at the guy with red hair as if he was the boss. Hell said the guy with red hair after staring hard at him he's all right leave him alone. So they all went out to the train.

On the way out to the train the little guy who had been winning said to Christ Christ are you going with us? And Christ said for a little ways but not far I got lots of trains to meet lots of dead men lots of them you wouldn't believe it. So they climbed on the train and Christ made just an easy little jump and swung right smack up on top of the engine. When the train started up everybody thought it was the train's whistle made the noise but it wasn't it was Christ perched up there and screaming that made the noise. So the train went rushing and screaming away with Christ perched on top of the engine his clothes trailing after him and hollering at the top of his voice. The train went so fast all you could see looking out of the window was a line between the sky and the earth and nothing else.

Pretty soon the train was in the middle of a big desert a hot yellow desert that shivered under the sun. Away off in the distance there was a cloud—a haze that was floating between the sky and the earth but nearer to the earth. And out of the haze was Christ coming up from Tucson. Christ floated there above the desert with purple robes drifting down and the heat waves swimming up around him.

Looking at Christ there above the desert he couldn't stand it any longer on the train. Dead men were on that train dead men or live men and he wasn't either so he had no business being there. He had no business being anywhere there was no place for him he was forgotten and abandoned and left forever alone. So he jumped out of the train right through the window and started running toward Christ.

The nightmare train went on through the sunlight its whistle screeching and the dead men inside laughing. But he was alone in the desert running running till his lungs squeaked running toward Christ who floated there in the heat with purple robes. He ran and he ran and he ran and finally he came up to Christ. He threw himself into the hot sand at the feet of Christ and began to cry.

xvii

He awakened as a man awakens out of a drunk—hazy-brained and foggy swimming slowly and painfully back toward reality. He awakened tapping with his head against his pillow. The tapping by now had become so much a part of awakening that the first glimmer of consciousness found him already tapping and later on when exhaustion overcame him and his mind began to grow dim and sleep crept over his body he was still tapping. He lay there not thinking of anything his brain aching and throbbing and his head tapping against the pillow. SOS. Help.

And then as his mind sharpened and began to think instead of only to feel he stopped his tapping and lay still. Something very important was happening. He had a new day nurse.

He could tell it the minute the door opened and she began to walk across the room. Her footsteps were light where those of his regular day nurse his old efficient fast-working day nurse were heavy. It took five steps to bring this new one to his bedside. That meant she was shorter than the regular nurse and probably younger too because the very vibration of her footsteps seemed gay and buoyant. It was the first time within his memory that the regular day nurse had not appeared to take care of him.

He lay very still very tense. This was like learning a new secret like opening a new world. Without a moment's hesitation the new nurse threw back his covers. And then like all of the others before her she stood quietly for a moment beside his bed. He knew she was staring down at him. He knew she must have been told what to expect. Yet the sight of him was probably so much worse than any description that she could do nothing for that first instant but stare. Then instead of hastily throwing the covers back over him as some of them did or running out of the room or standing and weeping and letting the tears fall against his chest she put her hand against his forehead. No one had ever done it before in just this way. Perhaps no one had been able to do it. It was like putting a hand near an open cancer something so terrible and sickening that no one could endure the thought much less the action. Yet this new nurse this nurse with the light happy step was not afraid.

She put her hand to his forehead and he felt that her hand was young and small and moist. She put her hand to his forehead and he tried to ripple his skin to show her how much he appreciated the way she had done it. It was like resting after a long long period of work. It was almost like sleep it was so lovely and soothing to have her hand against his head.

Then he began to think of the possibilities of this new nurse. For some reason the old one was gone. The old one had never understood what he was trying to do had never understood that he was trying with every ounce of his strength to talk to her. She had paid no attention at all to his tapping except to try to stop it. But she was gone and in her place he had a new nurse a young new nurse who was unafraid and gentle. How long he would have her no one could tell. She might leave the room and never come back again. But for the moment he had her and he knew that somehow she felt as he felt or she couldn't have put her hand so quickly to his forehead. If he could tap very firmly very clearly very plainly to her she might understand what no one else had considered worth trying to understand. She might understand that he was talking. The old nurse might return and he might never hear the footsteps of the new one again. If this new one went his last chance would go with her. He would go on through the rest of his life tapping tapping tapping with no one understanding that he was trying to work a miracle. The new nurse was his reprieve his one tiny opportunity in all the hours and weeks and years of his life.

He stiffened the muscles of his neck and prepared once more to start tapping his head against the pillow. But another strange thing was happening to arrest him. She had opened his nightshirt so that his breast was now naked to the air. She was moving the tip of her finger against the skin of his breast. For a moment he was merely puzzled unable to understand what she was doing. Then by concentrating all of his mind on the skin of his breast he began to understand that her finger was not travelling aimlessly. It was making a design against his skin. It was making the same design over and over again. He knew there was some purpose behind such repetition and he grew tense and alert to discover it. Like an eager dog spoken to by its master and trying very hard to be good and to understand he lay stiffly and concentrated on the design the nurse was making.

The first thing he noted about the design was that it had no curves. It was all straight lines and angles. It began with a straight line moving up and then it went down at an angle and then it came up again at an angle and then it went straight down and stopped. She repeated the design over and over now slowly now rapidly now slowly again. Sometimes she paused at the finish of the design and with the strange understanding that seemed to have sprung up between them he knew that her pauses were question marks that she was looking down at him and asking him if he understood and waiting for his response.

Each time she paused he shook his head and then she repeated the design once more and in the midst of this patient repetition the barrier between them suddenly broke down. With one quick rush of comprehension he understood what she was doing. She was tracing the letter M against the skin of his breast. He nodded quickly to tell her that he understood and she patted his forehead encouragingly as if to say you are remarkable you are wonderful how hard you try and how quickly you learn. Then she began to trace other letters.

The others came easier because he now understood what she was doing. He tightened the skin of his chest so that he could better receive the impression of her finger. Some of the letters she had to do only once he was so quick at getting them. He got the letter E and he nodded and the letter R and he nodded and again the R and then he got the letter Y and he nodded and there was a long pause. The rest of the letters tumbled into his mind in a perfect torrent. There was C and H and R and I and S and T and M and A and S and the whole thing spelled merry christmas.

Merry christmas merry christmas merry christmas.

Now he understood. The old nurse had left to spend the christmas holidays away from him and this new nurse this young lovely beautiful understanding new nurse was wishing him merry christmas. He nodded back at her frantically and his nod meant merry christmas to you merry christmas oh a merry merry christmas.

He thought to himself with a kind of hysterical happiness four years maybe five maybe six years I don't know how many years but I've been alone through all of them. He thought all my good work is gone all my way of keeping time has been forgotten but I don't care I am no longer alone. The years and years and years that he had been alone and now for the first time someone breaking through someone talking to him someone saying merry christmas. It was like a dazzling white light in the midst of darkness. It was like a great beautiful sound in the midst of silence. It was like an enormous laugh in the midst of death. It was christmas and someone had broken through and was wishing him merry christmas.

He heard the sound of sleigh bells and the crunch of snow and he saw candles in windows shining out

upon the snow warm and yellow and there were
wreaths of holly with red berries nestling like hot
coals against them and there was a clear sky overhead with clean blue-white little stars and there was
a feeling of peace and joy and relief because it was
christmas. He had been taken back into the world.

Merry christmas merry christmas merry christmas.

*Twas the night before christmas and all through
the house not a creature was stirring not even a
mouse. The stockings were hung by the chimney with
care in the hope that Saint Nicholas soon would be
there . . .*

In every christmas eve since he could remember
his mother had read the poem. Even after he was
much too old to believe in Santa Claus even after he
was a man maybe sixteen or seventeen years old still
she read the poem on christmas eve. In the beginning
when they were all together it was a wonderful thing
to hear her read it. They gathered in the living room
of the house in Shale City every christmas eve before
going to bed to listen to his mother read the poem.
His father would have been working late at the store
filling last minute christmas orders but at ten o'clock
the store closed and his father came home. It was
snowy and cold outside but the living room was always very snug and the pot-bellied coal-burning
stove would be glowing a warm dusty red around its
base.

Elizabeth being very young would be asleep in her
bed but Catherine would be there and his father and
mother and himself. Catherine would be in her night-
gown her discarded clothes in a heap near the stove

so they would be warm when she scrambled into them on christmas morning. They had no fireplace so the back of a chair served for a mantel. Hung on the chair were all of their stockings his father's his mother's Elizabeth's tiny little baby stocking Catherine's and his own. His father would be sitting back in the morris chair and Catherine would be snuggled against his legs. His mother would be in another chair with the opened book before her. Why his mother read the poem from a book no one could imagine except that it was a custom because they all knew it by heart. He would be on the floor huddled up with his hands around his legs staring at the door of the stove where the flames leaped behind isinglass windows.

The moon on the breast of the new-fallen snow gave a lustre of midday to objects below when what to my wandering eyes should appear but a miniature sleigh and eight tiny reindeer . . .

None of them ever forgot the poem. They could recite the whole thing any time of the year because it was the poem of christmas. As they listened to the poem it seemed that a delicious air of mystery stole over the room. Each member of the family had a little cache of gifts hidden somewhere in the house away from the others. It was very dishonorable for anyone to snoop on the day before christmas so no one ever did but there was no harm in speculating upon where the gifts might be hidden.

His mother's face as she read seemed to take on a warm happy glow. She was there in her own house with her family around her and they were all alive

201

and it was christmas eve and she was reading the poem she always read. It was so warm so secure so comforting to be home on christmas eve to be in a nice room with a good stove to feel somehow that here was a place in the wilderness a place forever safe a place that could never be changed could never be harmed could never be intruded upon. And now . . . he wondered about his mother tonight . . . his father gone and him away and it being christmas eve again. He wondered if somewhere in the world his mother at this moment might not be reading the poem. He could almost hear her voice thrill with excitement as she came to the climax.

Now Dasher now Dancer now Prancer and Vixen —on Comet on Cupid on Dunder and Blitzen—to the top of the porch to the top of the wall now dash away dash away dash away all . . .

Catherine's brown eyes were staring out now from her refuge by her father's legs staring out soberly yet glowing with little lights of excitement. A film had come over his father's eyes as if he had withdrawn a little and was imagining the scene in his own grownup way. His mother's face was animated her voice triumphant as she came to the thrilling part where Santa Claus slid down the chimney and nodded and set to work with his fat little belly shaking with laughter. And then where he put a finger to the side of his nose gave a nod and up the chimney arose. Then up to the roof where one almost could hear the scraping of the reindeers' little feet eager to be off to the next house.

He sprang to his sleigh to his team gave a whistle and away they all flew like down from a thistle. But I heard him exclaim ere he drove out of sight merry christmas to all and to all a good night. . .

They always sat quietly for a moment as his mother's voice died away. Nobody said a word because there was still something more to come. His mother laid aside the book of poems and reached for another book. She had a marker in the bible and she opened it now to the place that was marked and began to read again. She read the story of the little Christ-child of the baby Jesus and how he was born in a manger and how the star shone over Bethlehem and how the wise men traveled to him and how all the angels of heaven came near to the earth that night to sing of peace and the Christ-child and good will toward men.

He could hear her voice reading it off softly and reverently with the words coming like music from her lips. It was a funny thing he'd never read the bible story of christmas himself. He had only heard it as his mother read it to him. He couldn't remember the words but he could still see the pictures that used to come into his mind as his mother read. He knew the story by heart.

All the people were going to Bethlehem because it was tax time and they had to appear at the court house and register and pay up. They had been pouring in all day long and now it was night and the town was filled. Among those coming in was a man by the name of Joseph who was a carpenter in the town of Nazareth.

Joseph had to do a lot of chores before he could start out and Mary his wife was pregnant and couldn't help him so they were late. It was already dark by the time they came to the outskirts of Bethlehem. Joseph was leading their donkey and Mary poor wide-eyed girl was riding it and hoping they'd get settled soon because she was already feeling her pains and knew they didn't have much time. It was her first baby and she wasn't quite sure what to do when the time came.

As soon as they got into the town Joseph began making the rounds of cheap rooming houses. He wasn't much of a success at making money and they only had enough to pay their taxes and one night's rent. They went from rooming house to rooming house with Mary getting more frightened as her pains increased but the rooming houses were all filled because there were plenty of poor people even then and they had all beaten Joseph to the bargain places. Finally they counted their money and Joseph decided they would try the hotel. They could get a back bedroom and maybe he could do a little work around the place in the morning if their money didn't quite stretch out.

But the hotel was filled too.

Then Joseph began to talk very seriously to the hotel manager. See here he said I've come a long way and I've got my wife with me and she's going to have a baby. Look at her out there on the donkey you see she's just a kid and she's scared. She shouldn't have come in the first place only I couldn't leave her alone and I couldn't get anybody to stay with her overnight because they're all here paying their taxes. I've got to find a place for her to sleep and that's all there is to it.

The hotel manager looked out into the darkness and saw Mary's white anxious face there. She's a pretty kid he thought and scared too like her husband says. It'll be an awful mess if she has a baby on the premises people who can't afford them shouldn't have babies anyway but what are you going to do about it? All right he said to Joseph I guess I can find a place for you. See that passageway over there? Well go right on through it and you'll come to the barn. There's a manger at the far end. I'll have one of the boys throw down some hay and it'll be comfortable. I don't mind telling you I hope very much she doesn't have her baby here tonight because it'll upset my guests if she screams and they're all very high-class people including three Roman congressmen. But go ahead.

Joseph said thanks and started off toward Mary. Oh I almost forgot yelled the hotel keeper after him don't light any fires out there in the barn because in my insurance it says they're forbidden and I can't afford to have my insurance cancelled. Joseph hollered that he would be careful and the hotel keeper went back into the warm and stood in front of the fire and thought it's a shame people having kids all over the place it's good and chilly tonight too I do hope she doesn't make a fuss.

Back in the manger Joseph lighted a lantern and fixed up a nice bed on the hay and Mary lay down on the bed and had her baby. It was a boy. They wrapped it up in a blanket they had brought especially for it and Mary who was a good strong girl held the baby real tight against her. I was almost sure it would be a boy she said to Joseph. What are we going to name it? Joseph asked her. I think I would like to name it Jesus she said. She looked quickly down at the baby and back to Joseph the fright all gone from her eyes and a smile on her lips.

But Joseph staring down at the two of them didn't smile. Mary noticed this and said Joseph what's the matter you don't look happy it's a fine baby look at its chubby hands why don't you smile? And Joseph said there's a light around the head of our baby a shine that is soft like moonlight. Mary nodded as if she weren't a bit surprised and said I think there must be a light like that around the heads of all newborn babies they're so fresh from heaven. And Joseph said in a kind of sick voice as if he had suddenly lost something there's a light around your head too Mary.

Out in the hills beyond Bethlehem a sheep herder was trying to get a little rest. The sheep were all lying down and there had been such a hub-bub in Bethlehem from so many people coming from all directions that he was sure the wolves were scared back into the hills so there wasn't any risk in him getting forty winks. He lay there sleeping when suddenly he woke up with a light shining in his face. He opened his eyes and started to look around. For a minute he couldn't see a thing because he was blinded by starlight. When he finally got himself organized he saw a star hanging low in the sky over Bethlehem a star so near you could almost reach out and touch it and so bright it lighted the whole town. The walls and house-tops of Bethlehem stood out sharp and clear and white and on the hillside around him he could see his sheep like little lumps of silver against the earth.

Then he heard sounds on the road and looked off to the left. Coming around the foot of the hill where the road turned into Bethlehem were three camels with three riders. The sheep herder could tell by their clothes that they were out-of-staters of some kind. He could see the silver decorations of their saddles reflecting back the light of the star over Bethlehem. He watched them for a minute thinking that they looked pretty well off to be having to pay taxes and then he heard the music. The air was filled with angels singing in the starlight. This night they sang in the town of Bethlehem there is born a little baby who shall be the saviour of the world. He is the prince of peace and the son of god and his name is Jesus. Peace on earth and good will toward men. Rejoice everyone and sing with the angels for this night a saviour is born. Peace peace peace on earth and good will toward men.

The sheep herder who was not used to angels singing in the sky above the place he worked and so knew it must be some kind of a miracle got down on his knees and lowered his head in prayer. He didn't look up for a long while even though he was afraid that all the noise might startle his sheep and cause him to spend half the night rounding them up again.

Away off in Rome a man in a palace stirred in his sleep. He almost awakened and then drowsed off again wondering in his dreams why he was nervous. In the manger in Bethlehem Mary listened to the angels and didn't seem to feel as happy as when she first saw her child. She stared right through the wise men who had come with presents. She hugged her baby closer. Her eyes were filled with pain and fear for the little baby.

xviii

When he finally forced his mind away from thoughts
of christmas of merry christmas he began to tap once
more. Only this time he tapped firmly with vigor
full of hope and confidence for he saw that this new
nurse this lovely new nurse was thinking as hard as
he was and of the same thing. He knew as plainly
as if she had told him that she was determined to
batter down the silence which stood between him as
a dead man and him as a live man. Since she had
already thought of a way to speak to him he knew
that she would pay attention when he tried to speak
to her. The others had been too busy or too tired or
else not bright enough to see what he was doing.
They had taken his tapping as a nervous habit as a
disease as the whim of a child as a symptom of insanity as anything but what it really was as anything
but a cry from the darkness a voice from the dead a
wail in the silence for friendship and someone to

talk to. But the new nurse would understand and help him.

He tapped very carefully very slowly to show her that he had a method in what he was doing. Just as she had repeated the design of the letter M on his chest over and over again so he now tapped his distress signal back to her. But slowly . . . so slowly. Dot dot dot   dot dot   dot dot dot. S O S. H e l p. Over and over again he repeated it. Once in a while he would stop at the completion of the signal. That was his question mark just as her pauses had been question marks. He would stop and try to make all that was visible of him—his hair and half his forehead above the mask—take on an air of expectancy. Then when he received no sign from her he would do it again. And all the while he tapped he was conscious of her near him watching and thinking.

After a long period of waiting and watching and thinking she began to do things. She did them very deliberately so deliberately that even her movements seemed thoughtful. First she slipped the urinal in under the covers touching it against his body so that he could recognize it. He shook his head. She took the urinal away and slipped the bed pan against him. He shook his head. She took the bed pan away. There was no hesitation between her movements now. It seemed that she had each move figured out before she finished the last one. She was working skillfully and intelligently to eliminate all possible causes for his tapping one by one with no pauses in between. He knew that during the time she had stood beside him watching and thinking she had made up

her mind to a plan and now was putting it into effect
with as little nonsense as possible.

She took the blanket off him leaving him with only
a sheet for covering. He shook his head. She put the
blanket back and threw another one over it to give
him more covers than before. He shook his head.
He had stopped tapping now waiting alertly until
she was through with her plan. She took the covers
off him entirely and adjusted the position of the
breathing tube in his throat. He shook his head. She
patted the bandage over the hole in his side. He
shook his head. He shook his head and marveled
that he had the sense left to do it because he was so
charged with excitement that he could scarcely think.
She lifted the nightshirt that covered him and began
gently to rub his body. He shook his head. She threw
the covers over him again and moved toward the
head of the bed. She rubbed his forehead soothingly.
He shook his head. She smoothed his hair back and
scratched his scalp and massaged it with her knuckles.
He shook his head. She loosened the cord that held
the mask over his face. He shook his head. She lifted
the mask up and fanned it gently to let the air in
and be sure it wasn't sticking. He shook his head.
She replaced the bandage and stopped everything. He
could feel her standing beside the head of the bed
looking down at him attentively as alert and eager
as he was himself. She had done everything she
could think of and now she was standing there quietly as if to say it's your turn now please try hard to
tell me and I will try hard to understand.

He began to tap again.

It seemed to him that he stopped breathing. It
seemed that his heart stopped and the blood in his

body turned solid. It seemed that the only living moving thing in the whole world was his head as it tapped tapped tapped against his pillow. He knew it was now or never. There was no good in fooling himself now. This minute this instant this very second everything was about to be decided. Never again would he have a nurse such as this one. She might turn and walk out of the room in five minutes and never return. When she walked away she would carry his life with her she would carry madness and loneliness and all his godforsaken silent screams and she would never know it she would never hear the screams. She would simply go and ever after he would be forgotten. She was loneliness and friendship she was life and death and she stood now waiting quietly for him to tell her what he wanted.

While he tapped he was praying in his heart. He had never paid much attention to praying before but now he was doing it saying oh please god make her understand what I'm trying to tell her. I've been alone so long god I've been here for years and years suffocating smothering dead while alive like a man who has been buried in a casket deep in the ground and awakens and screams I'm alive I'm alive I'm alive let me out open the lid dig away the dirt please merciful christ help me only there's no one to hear him and so he's dead. I know you're very busy god I know there are millions of people praying to you every minute every hour for something they need I know there are a lot of important people who are after you for big things that are all tied up with nations and continents and maybe even the whole world. I know all these things god and I don't blame you if you get behind on your orders nobody's perfect but what I want is such a little thing. If I were asking you for something big something like a million dollars or a private yacht or a skyscraper I could understand if I didn't get it because there are only so many dollars and so many yachts and so many skyscrapers. But I only want you should take a tiny little idea that is in my mind and put it into her mind two maybe three feet away. That's all I want god. The idea is so small so light that a humming bird could carry it a moth a mayfly the breath of air that comes from the mouth of a baby. It won't take any time and it means I can't tell you what to me. Honestly I wouldn't ask you god only this is such a little thing. It's such a little thing . . .

He felt her finger against his forehead.

He nodded.

He felt her finger tap four times against his forehead.

That is the letter H he thought only she doesn't know it she's got no idea she's just tapping there to test if that's what I want.

He nodded.

He nodded so hard his neck ached and his head seemed to whirl. He nodded so hard the whole bed shook.

Oh thank you god he thought she got it you put the idea where I asked you should thank you. Thank you thank you thank you.

He felt her hand pressed against his forehead reassuringly for just a minute. Then he got the rapidly receding vibrations of her footsteps going away. He knew she was running from the room to tell them. The door slammed behind her. The sound quivered against his bedsprings like an electric shock. She was gone.

He lay back surprised to find how exhausted he was. It was like he had worked three nights in a row at the bakery during the summer when he couldn't get any sleep in the daytime. The breath was gone out of him and his head throbbed and every muscle in his body was sore. Yet inside he was all confetti and high-flying flags and double-time band music that marched up and up straight into the face of the sun. He had done it he had succeeded the thing was accomplished and even though he lay perfectly still perfectly exhausted it seemed he could see the whole world lying below him. There was no telling it there was no thinking it there was no imagining it he was so happy.

It was as if all the people in the world the whole two billion of them had been against him pushing the lid of the coffin down on him tamping the dirt solid against the lid rearing great stones above the dirt to keep him in the earth. Yet he had risen. He had lifted the lid he had thrown away the dirt he had tossed the granite aside like a snowball and now he was above the surface he was standing in the air he was leaping with every step miles above the earth. He was like nobody else who had ever lived. He had done so much he was like god.

The doctors who brought their friends in to see him would no longer say here is a man who has lived without arms legs ears eyes nose mouth isn't it wonderful? They would say here is a man who can think here is a man who lay in his bed with only a cut of meat to hold him together and yet he thought of a way to talk. Listen to him speak. You see his mind is unaffected he speaks like you and me he is a person he has identity he is part of the world. And he is part of the world only because he all by himself with perhaps the aid of a prayer and a god figured out a way to speak. Look at him and then let us ask you if this isn't even more wonderful than all the splendid operations we have performed upon his stump?

He knew now that he had never been really happy in his whole life. There had been times when he had thought he was happy but none of them were like this. There was the time when all year long he had wanted an erector set and when at christmas time he got it. That was probably as happy as he had ever been while he was a kid. There was the time when Kareen told him she loved him and that was as happy as he had ever been up to the time the shell exploded and blew him out of the world. But this happiness this new wild frantic happiness was greater than anything he could conceive. It was a thing so absolute so towering so out of this world that it hit him almost like delirium. His legs that were smashed and gone got up and danced. His arms that were rotted these five six seven years swung fantastically free at his sides to keep time with the dance. The eyes they had taken from him looked up from whatever garbage heap they had been consigned to and saw all the beauties of the world. The ears that were shattered and full of silence rang suddenly with music. The mouth that had been hacked away from his face and now was filled with dust returned to sing. Because he had done it. He had accomplished the impossible. He had spoken to them like god out of a cloud out of a thick cloud and now he was floating on top of the cloud and he was a man again.

And the nurse . . .

He could imagine her running through the halls. He could hear her clattering like a noisy ghost through the halls of death. He could feel her running from ward to ward from the ward of the cripples to the ward of the deaf men to the ward of the blind men to the ward of the voiceless men summoning all the people of the hospital screaming out to them the news of the wonder that had happened. He could hear her voice as she told them that up in a little room away from the rest of the hospital a lid had been lifted from a coffin a stone had been rolled away from a tomb and a dead man was tapping and talking. Never before in the world had the dead spoken never since Lazarus and Lazarus didn't say anything. Now he would tell them everything. He would speak from the dead. He would talk for the dead. He would tell all the secrets of the dead. And while he thought of what he would tell them the nurse was running running running through wards and corridors from floor to floor from basement to attic all through that great place from which so many dead had gone. She was trumpeting through the hospital like the angel Gabriel telling them to come and to listen to the voice of the dead.

While he waited for all the people she had summoned to come to him he could feel their presence as an actor must feel the presence of a thousand people in that moment before the curtain goes up. He could feel the vibrations of their footsteps dozens of them as they thronged into his room. He could feel his bed jostled back and forth as they pressed against it in their eagerness. The springs of his bed seemed to send up a constant low hum as his guests shifted for positions to get a better view of the dead man who was speaking. The temperature of the room became so much warmer that he could almost feel the heat of their massed bodies against the skin of his neck and the half of his forehead that was naked above the mask.

Then the door opened. He felt the vibration of a footstep a light one the nurse's footstep. He strained to feel the rest. Then came the vibrations of another footstep this one heavier belonging to a man. He waited for the rest he waited for the hum of his bedsprings. But everything was quiet. Everything was still. There was no one in the room for the great thing that was about to happen except him and his nurse and this heavy-footed stranger. No one at all but the three of them. He felt an odd pang of disappointment that they should consider such a great event so lightly. And then he remembered the thing that was even more important than crowds. He lay there stiff quiet more like a dead man than he had ever been before. He lay there waiting to receive his response.

A finger came out of the darkness a finger so enormous that it shattered against his forehead like the crash of a pile driver. It echoed inside his brain like thunder in a cave. The finger began to tap . . .

.— — .... .— —
W H A T

—.. ——
D O

... .. ö ..── ──
Y O U

.── ── .── .── .── ──
W A N T

What do you want?

When he made out the question when he was sure
he had translated it right he grew very quiet for a
moment. It was like sitting in a silent room waiting
for someone very important someone for whom you
have been waiting a long while and then suddenly
hearing a knock on the door. For just a minute you
hesitate wondering who it might be and what does
he want and why did he come. For just a second
you're scared because although you've waited for
years you really never expected the knock. Then
you get up and go over and open the door just a
little at first to prepare yourself for the shock of
disappointment at discovering it isn't the person
you've been wanting. But when you find that the
impossible has happened that the visitor you've been
praying for has arrived you're so relieved and surprised you don't know exactly what to say or how
to begin it.

What did he want?

It was as if someone who longed for the sea and a ship were suddenly given his ship and then asked where he wanted to go. He hadn't ever really expected the ship so he had spent all his time wishing for it and no time figuring out what to do with it after he got it. He was the same way. He had never really expected to break through it had been so long and he'd had such trouble trying to make them understand. The whole thing had been just an idea it had been something to hope for and work for and the more difficult it got the more important it became until in the end it was driving him almost crazy. But up to an hour ago he had never imagined himself in the position of actually breaking through. Now he had accomplished it. The thing was done and they were asking him what he wanted. And even though all that was left of his life seemed to depend on answering them he couldn't organize his thoughts enough to make sense to himself much less to anyone else.

Then he thought about it in another way. Maybe it wasn't so much a question of what he wanted as what they could give him. That was it. And what could they give him? He began to resent the question itself and the way they asked it and the ignorance that lay behind it. Who did they think they were and what did they think he wanted that they could give him? Did they think he would ask for an ice cream cone? Did they think he would ask for a good book and an open fire and a cat purring? Did they think he would ask to go to a movie and after that to a soda parlor for a nice cool drink of lemonade? Did they think he would ask for dancing lessons or a pair of binoculars or a course in piano lessons imagine how surprised your friends will be?

Maybe they thought he wanted a new suit or a silk shirt. Maybe they expected him to complain that the bed was a little hard and please bring me a glass of water. Maybe they thought he would ask for a change of diet. The coffee you've been pouring into my tube lately needs a little more sugar it tastes bitter to my intestines so add half a teaspoonful of sugar and stir it well please. The hash is too wet and it needs some seasoning. I think I would like some fudge. Next time you shove grub through that tube stick in a piece of fudge not sugary not too strong of chocolate but smooth and a little warm I've been waiting all these years and tapping all these months because I love fudge so much.

They should know what he wanted the silly bastards and they should know they couldn't give it to him. He wanted the things they took for granted the things nobody could ever give him. He wanted eyes to see with. Two eyes to see sunlight and moonlight and blue mountains and tall trees and little ants and houses that people live in and flowers opening in the morning and snow on the ground and streams running and trains coming and going and people walking and a puppy dog playing with an old shoe worrying it and growling at it and backing away from it and frowning and wiggling its bottom and taking the shoe very seriously. He wanted a nose so that he could smell rain and burning wood and cooking food and the faint perfume that stays in the air after a girl has passed by. He wanted a mouth so he could eat and talk and laugh and taste and kiss. He wanted arms and legs so that he could work and walk and be like a man like a living thing.

What did he want what was there for him to want what was there left that anybody could give him?

It came over him rushing and howling like a torrent of water from behind a dam that has broken. He wanted to get out. He could feel his heart speed up and his flesh tighten at the thought. He wanted to get out. He wanted to get out so that he could feel the taste of fresh air against his skin and imagine even though he couldn't smell that it came from the sea or the mountains or the cities or the farmlands. He wanted to get out so that he could feel people around him. It didn't matter that he couldn't see them or hear them or talk with them. If he were out he would know that at least he was among them that he was not shut up in a room away from them. It wasn't right that a man should be shut up in a room. It wasn't right that he should be a prisoner forever. A man needed to be among other men. Every living thing needed to be among its own kind. He was a man a part of mankind and he wanted to be taken out so that he could sense other men around him.

Let me out he thought that's all I want. I've been lying here for years and years in a room in a bed in a little covering of skin. Now I want out. I've got to get out. You can't keep a man here like this. He's got to be doing something in order to be sure he's still alive. I'm like a prisoner here and you've got no right to keep me because I've done no wrong. One room one bed like in a jail like in an asylum like in a grave with six feet of earth above. You don't realize how a man can stand only so much of this without going crazy. I'm suffocating and I can't suffocate any longer I can't stand it. If I had arms I could move I could push I could widen the walls I could throw back the covers I could get into a bigger place. If I had a voice I could yell and holler for help I could talk to myself and be some company to myself. If I had legs I could run I could get away I could come out into the open where there is air where there is room where I'm not in a hole and smothering. But I haven't got any of these things I can't do any of these things so you must help me. You must help me quick because inside I'm going crazy I'm going insane I'm suffering like you'll never know. Inside me I scream and howl and push and fight for room for air for escape from the smothering. So let me out where I can feel air and sense people. Please let me out so I can have room to breathe in. Let me out of here and take me back into the world.

He was about to tap to them in a flood of dots and dashes when it came over him that there might be difficulties. After all he wasn't an ordinary guy to be released from an ordinary prison to lead an ordinary life. He was a very unusual case. All his life no matter where he was there would have to be people taking care of him. That meant money and he didn't have any money and so he would be a burden to people. The government or whoever it was taking care of him probably didn't have any money to throw around humoring a guy spending a fortune taking care of him just so he could feel air on the outside and the presence of people around him. That might make sense to some people but you could never get the government to understand it. The government would say he is nuts who ever heard of a guy without arms legs eyes ears nose mouth getting any fun out of being around people he can't see or hear or talk to? The government would say the whole thing is a crazy idea and the hell with it he's better off where he is and besides it costs too much dough.

And then he realized that he had it in his own power to make money plenty of it enough to pay his own expenses and the expenses of the people who took care of him too. Instead of being a burden and a bother to the government he could even make money for them. People were always willing to pay to see a curiosity they were always interested in terrible sights and probably nowhere on the face of the earth was there any living thing quite so terrible as he was. Once he saw an exhibition of a man who was turning to stone. You could tap a coin against his arm and it sounded as if you were tapping it against marble the coin would ring so. That was terrible enough but not nearly so terrible as he was. Yet that man turning to stone was paying his own way and making enough money to pay somebody to take care of him to boot. He could do the same thing. If they would only let him out he would be able to take care of everything.

He would be doing good too in a roundabout way. He would be an educational exhibit. People wouldn't learn much about anatomy from him but they would learn all there was to know about war. That would be a great thing to concentrate war in one stump of a body and to show it to people so they could see the difference between a war that's in newspaper headlines and liberty loan drives and a war that is fought out lonesomely in the mud somewhere a war between a man and a high explosive shell. Suddenly

he took fire with the idea he got so excited over it
he forgot about his longing for air and people this
new idea was so wonderful. He would make an exhibit of himself to show all the little guys what would
happen to them and while he was doing it he would
be self-supporting and free. He would do a favor to
everybody including himself. He would show himself
to the little guys and to their mothers and fathers
and brothers and sisters and wives and sweethearts
and grandmothers and grandfathers and he would
have a sign over himself and the sign would say here
is war and he would concentrate the whole war into
such a small piece of meat and bone and hair that
they would never forget it as long as they lived.

He began to tap that he wanted out. His mind ran
way ahead of his tapping but he kept on tapping just
the same. What did he want? He'd tell them what he
wanted the goddam fools. He'd tell them he'd tap it
out to them word by word he'd remember every bit
of it and put it down in dots and dashes and then
they would know. As he tapped he thought faster.
He grew angrier and more excited and he tapped
faster and faster trying to keep up with the words
that were pounding on the inside of his mind the
words he could finally use all the words he had
thought of in all the years he had lain silent for he
was talking now for the first time he had learned how
and he was talking to someone outside.

Let me out he tapped let me out of here let me
out. I won't give you any trouble. I won't be any
care. I can earn my keep. I can do a job like anybody else. Take off my nightshirt and build a glass
case for me and take me down to the places where
people are having fun where they are on the lookout

for freakish things. Take me in my glass case to the beaches and the country fairs and the church bazaars and the circuses and the travelling carnivals.

You could do a wonderful business with me I could pay you for the trouble. You could give them a good spiel. They've heard of the half-man half-woman. They've heard of the bearded woman and the thin man and the midget. They've seen the human mermaids and the wild men from Borneo and the meat-eating girl from the Congo throw her a fish and watch her snap for it. They've seen the man who writes with his toes and the man who walks on his hands and the Siamese twins and those little rows of unborn babies pickled in alcohol.

But they've seen nothing like this. This will be the goddamndest dime's worth a man ever had. This will be a sensation in the show world and whoever sponsors my tour will be a new Barnum and have fine notices in all the newspapers because I am something you can really holler about. I am something you can push with a money back guarantee. I am the deadman-who-is-alive. I am the live-man-who-is-dead. If they won't come into our tent with that build-up then I am something more. I'm the man who made the world safe for democracy. If they won't fall for that then for Christ sake they're no men. Let them join the army because the army makes men.

Take me along country roads and stop by every farmhouse and every field and ring a dinner gong so that the farmers and their wives and their children and their hired men and women can see me. Say to the farmers here is something I'll bet you haven't seen before. Here is something you can't plow under. Here is something that will never grow and flower. The

manure you plow into your fields is filthy enough but
here is something less than manure because it won't
die and decay and nourish even a weed. Here is
something so terrible that if it were born to a mare or
a heifer or a sow or a ewe you would kill it on the
spot but you can't kill this because it is a human
being. It has a brain. It is thinking all the time. Believe it or not this thing thinks and it is alive and it
goes against every rule of nature although nature
doesn't make it so. You know what made it so.
Look at it medals real medals probably of solid
gold. Lift up the top of the case and you'll know
what made it so. It stinks of glory.

Take me into the places where men work and
make things. Take me there and say boys here is a
cheap way to get by. Maybe times are bad and your
salaries are low. Don't worry boys because there is
always a way to cure things like that. Have a war
and then prices go up and wages go up and everybody makes a hell of a lot of money. There'll be
one along pretty soon boys so don't get impatient.
It'll come and then you'll have your chance.

Either way you win. If you don't have to fight
why you stay at home and make sixteen bucks a day
working in the shipyards. And if they draft you why
you've got a good chance of coming back without
so many needs. Maybe you'll need only one shoe
instead of two that's saving money. Maybe you'll be
blind and if you are why then you never need worry
about the expense of glasses. Maybe you'll be lucky
like me. Look at me close boys I don't need anything.
A little broth or something three times a day and
that's all. No shoes no socks no underwear no shirt
no gloves no hat no necktie no collar-buttons no vest

no coat no movies no vaudeville no football not even a shave. Look at me boys I have no expenses at all. You're suckers boys. Get on the gravy train. I know what I'm talking about. I used to need all the things that you need right now. I used to be a consumer. I've consumed a lot in my time. I've consumed more shrapnel and gunpowder than any living man. So don't get blue boys because you'll have your chance there'll be another war along pretty soon and then maybe you'll be lucky like me.

Take me into the schoolhouses all the schoolhouses in the world. Suffer little children to come unto me isn't that right? They may scream at first and have nightmares at night but they'll get used to it because they've got to get used to it and it's best to start them young. Gather them around my case and say here little girl here little boy come and take a look at your daddy. Come and look at yourself. You'll be like that when you grow up to be great big strong men and women. You'll have a chance to die for your country. And you may not die you may come back like this. Not everybody dies little kiddies.

Closer please. You over there against the blackboard what's the matter with you? Quit crying you silly little girl come over here and look at the nice man the nice man who was a soldier boy. You remember him don't you? Don't you remember little crybaby how you waved flags and saved tinfoil and put your savings in thrift stamps? Of course you do you silly. Well here's the soldier you did it for.

Come on youngsters take a nice look and then we'll go into our nursery rhymes. New nursery rhymes for new times. Hickory dickory dock my daddy's nuts from shellshock. Humpty dumpty thought he was wise till gas came along and burned out his eyes. A dillar a dollar a ten o'clock scholar blow off his legs and then watch him holler. Rocka-bye baby in the treetop don't stop a bomb or you'll probably flop. Now I lay me down to sleep my bomb-proof cellar's good and deep but if I'm killed before I wake remember god it's for your sake amen.

Take me into the colleges and universities and academies and convents. Call the girls together all the healthy beautiful young girls. Point down to me and say here girls is your father. Here is that boy who was strong last night. Here is your little son your baby son the fruit of your love the hope of your future. Look down on him girls so you won't forget him. See that red gash there with mucus hanging to it? That was his face girls. Here girls touch it don't be afraid. Bend down and kiss it. You'll have to wipe your lips afterward because they will have a strange rotten stuff on them but that's all right be-cause a lover is a lover and here is your lover.

Call all the young men together and say here is your brother here is your best friend here you are young men. This is a very interesting case young men because we know there is a mind buried down there. Technically this thing is living meat like that tissue we kept alive all last summer in the lab. But this is a different cut of meat because it also con-tains a brain. Now listen to me closely young gen-tlemen. That brain is thinking. Maybe it's thinking about music. Maybe it has a great symphony all thought out or a mathematical formula that would change the world or a book that would make peo-ple kinder or the germ of an idea that would save a hundred million people from cancer. This is a very interesting problem young gentlemen because if this brain does hold such secrets how in the world are we ever going to find out? In any event there you are young gentlemen breathing and thinking and dead like a frog under chloroform with its stomach laid open so that its heartbeat may be seen so quiet so helpless but yet alive. There is your future and your sweet wild dreams there is the thing your sweethearts loved and there is the thing your leaders urged it to be. Think well young gentlemen. Think sharply young gentlemen and then we will go back to our studies of the barbarians who sacked Rome.

Take me wherever there are parliaments and diets and congresses and chambers of statesmen. I want to be there when they talk about honor and justice and making the world safe for democracy and four-teen points and the self determination of peoples. I want to be there to remind them I haven't got a tongue to stick into the cheek I haven't got either. But the statesmen have tongues. The statesmen have cheek. Put my glass case upon the speaker's desk and every time the gavel descends let me feel its vibration through my little jewel case. Then let them speak of trade policies and embargoes and new colonies and old grudges. Let them debate the men-ace of the yellow race and the white man's burden and the course of empire and why should we take all this crap off Germany or whoever the next Germany is. Let them talk about the South American market and why so-and-so is beating us out of it and why our merchant marine can't compete and oh what the hell let's send a good stiff note. Let them talk more munitions and airplanes and battleships and tanks and gases why of course we've got to have them we can't get along without them how in the world could we protect the peace if we didn't have them? Let them form blocs and alliances and mutual assistance pacts and guarantees of neutrality. Let them draft notes and ultimatums and protests and accusations.

But before they vote on them before they give the order for all the little guys to start killing each other let the main guy rap his gavel on my case and point down at me and say here gentlemen is the only issue before this house and that is are you for this thing here or are you against it. And if they are against it why goddam them let them stand up like men and vote. And if they are for it let them be hanged and drawn and quartered and paraded through the streets in small chopped up little bits and thrown out into the fields where no clean animal will touch them and let their chunks rot there and may no green thing ever grow where they rot.

Take me into your churches your great towering cathedrals that have to be rebuilt every fifty years because they are destroyed by war. Carry me in my glass box down the aisles where kings and priests and brides and children at their confirmation have gone so many times before to kiss a splinter of wood from a true cross on which was nailed the body of a man who was lucky enough to die. Set me high on your altars and call on god to look down upon his murderous little children his dearly beloved little children. Wave over me the incense I can't smell. Swill down the sacramental wine I can't taste. Drone out the prayers I can't hear. Go through the old holy gestures for which I have no legs and no arms. Chorus out the hallelujas I can't sing. Bring them out loud and strong for me your hallelujas all of them for me because I know the truth and you don't you fools. You fools you fools you fools . . .

He felt the vibrations of heavy feet leaving the room. The man who had come in and tapped the question and who had stood listening to his reply for how long he couldn't imagine had gone. He was alone with the nurse again. He was left alone to wonder.

He began to have misgivings. Just as he had always suspected himself of some mistake in his count of time so now he felt wild little ripples of fear shudder through his flesh. He had been so eager to tap that perhaps his message hadn't made sense. Perhaps he had made a mistake in remembering the code so that his words came out as a jumble of letters with no meaning. His thoughts had rushed through his head so tumultuously that perhaps he hadn't got them down in order clearly and sanely. Perhaps ten thousand other possibilities had come between him and the message he was bleeding inside to give them. Or perhaps the man had just gone away to talk to his superior and would soon return with an answer.

That was it. Oh please god that must be it he was sure of it. The man would return soon with an answer. All he had to do was lie back and rest he was so tired. It seemed to him that he was lying in some kind of dream coma like a man who has spent all his emotions in one wild drunk and afterward is simply sick and disgusted and sure of the worst. He had been tapping now for weeks months maybe years he couldn't tell because the tapping had taken the place of time for him and all his energies had gone into it all his energies and all his hopes and all his life.

He stiffened.

The vibrations were coming toward him again. The man was returning with an answer. Great merciful god thank you here it is here it is my answer. Here is my triumph here is my return from the dead here is life vibrating against the floor singing in my bedsprings singing like all the angels in heaven.

A finger began to tap against his forehead.

•— — •••• •— —
W H A T

••• •• •—
Y O U

•— ••• —•—
A S K

•• •••
I S

•— —• —•—• •— •• —• •••—
A G A I N S T

234

REGULATIONS
WHO
ARE
YOU

The tapping went on against his forehead but he paid no more attention to it. Everything in his mind went suddenly blank hollow completely quiet. A moment of this and then he began to think about the message to make certain there was no mistake that it meant exactly what it said. And he knew it did.

He could almost hear the wail of pain that went up from his heart. It was a sharp terrible personal pain the kind of pain that comes only when someone to whom you have never done any harm turns on you and says goodbye goodbye forever without any reason for doing it. Without any reason at all.

He had done nothing to them. He wasn't to blame for the trouble he was causing yet they were drawing the curtain around him stuffing him back into the womb back into the grave saying to him goodbye don't bother us don't come back to life the dead should stay dead and we are done with you.

But why?

He had hurt no one. He had tried to give them as little trouble as possible. He was a great care that was true but he hadn't intentionally become so. He wasn't a thief or a drunkard or a liar or a murderer.

He was a man a guy no worse no better than anybody else. He was just a guy who'd had to go to war
who'd been bad hurt and now was trying to get out
from his prison to feel fresh cool air on his skin to
sense the color and movement of people around him.
That was all he wanted. And to him who had harmed
nobody they were saying goodnight goodbye stay
where you are don't give us any trouble you are beyond life you are beyond death you are even beyond
hope you are gone you are finished forever goodnight
and goodbye.

In one terrible moment he saw the whole thing.
They wanted only to forget him. He was upon their
conscience so they had abandoned him they had
forsaken him. They were the only people in the world
who could help him. They were his last court of ap-
peal. He might rage and storm and howl against their
verdict but it would do him no good. They had decided. Nothing could change them. He was completely at their mercy and they had no mercy. For him
there was no hope. He might just as well come face
to face with the truth.

Every moment of his life since he had awakened
into the darkness and dumbness and terror every
moment of it had been concentrated upon the time
some day some year when he would break through
to them. Now he had done it. He had broken
through and they had refused him. Before even in
his most terrible moments there had been a vague
hope that kept him going. It had prevented him
from going stark raving crazy it had shined like a
glow in the distance toward which he never stopped
moving. Now the glow was gone and there was
nothing left. There was no reason for him to fool

himself about it any longer. These people didn't want him. Darkness desertion loneliness silence horror unending horror—these were his life from now on without a single ray of hope to lighten his sufferings. They were his whole future. It was for them that his mother had borne him. Curse her curse the world curse the sunlight curse god curse every decent thing on earth. God damn them god damn them and torture them as he was being tortured. God give them darkness and silence and dumbness and helplessness and horror and fear the great towering terrible fear that was with him now the desolation and the loneliness that would be with him forever.

No.

No no no.

He wouldn't let them do it.

It was impossible for one human being to do this to another. No one could be so cruel. They didn't understand that was all he hadn't made it plain enough to them. He couldn't give up now he must go on and on until they understood because they were good people they were good kindly people and they needed only to understand.

He began to tap again.

He began to tap again and to tell them pleadingly haltingly humbly that please he wanted out. He wanted to feel air against him the fresh clean air outside a hospital. Please understand. He wanted the feel of people of his own kind free and happy. There really wasn't any good reason except that. The thing about showing him in a case forget that it was just a way to raise money and make it easier on them. Only that. He was lonesome. That was all just lonesome. There were no more reasons he could give them.

There was nothing he could do except to try to let them know that inside the skin that covered his body there was so much terror so much loneliness that it was only right they should permit him such a small thing as the freedom he could pay for.

As he tapped he felt the nurse's hand against his forehead stroking him soothing him. He thought to himself I wish I could see her face. It must be a beautiful face she has such beautiful hands. Then against the stump of his left arm he felt a sudden wet coolness. The man who had tapped his answer was applying an alcoholic swab. Oh god he thought I know what that means don't do it please don't. Then he felt the sharp deadly prick of the needle. They were giving him dope again.

Oh god he thought they won't even let me talk. They won't even listen to me any more. All they want is to make a madman out of me so that whenever I tap my messages to them they can say he's only crazy don't pay any attention to him poor fellow he's nuts. That's what they're trying to do god they're trying to drive me crazy and I've fought so hard I've been so strong that the only way they can do it is by giving me dope.

He felt himself sinking back back into the place where they wanted to thrust him. He felt the tingle of his own flesh and he began to see the vision. He saw the yellow sand and he saw the heat waves coming up from it. Above the heat waves he saw Christ in his flowing robes and his crown of thorns with the blood dripping from them. He saw Christ quivering in the desert heat coming up from Tucson. And far off in the distance he heard a woman's voice crying my son my little boy my son . . .

In sheer terrible desperation he shut out the voice he pushed the vision away. Not yet. Not yet. He wasn't through. He would talk to them he would keep on tapping. The muscles of his body were turning to water but he would keep on tapping. He would not let them lower the lid to his coffin. He would scream and claw and fight as any man should do when they are burying him alive. In his last moment of consciousness in his last moment of life he would still fight he would still tap. He would keep on and on and on tapping all the while tapping when he was asleep tapping when he was doped tapping when he was in pain tapping forever. They might not answer him they might ignore him but at least they would never be able to forget that as long as he lived here was a man who was talking to them talking to them all the time.

His taps came slower and slower and the vision swam toward him and he pushed it away and it swam toward him again. The woman's voice faded in and out like something that is carried on the wind. But still he tapped.

He was tapping why? why? why?

Why didn't they want him? Why were they shutting the lid of the coffin against him? Why didn't they want him to speak? Why didn't they want him to be seen? Why didn't they want him to be free? It was five maybe six years now since he had been blown out of the world. The war must be over by now. No war could last that long killing so many people there weren't enough people to kill. If the war was over then all the dead had been buried and all the prisoners had been released. Why shouldn't he be released too? Why not unless they figured him as one of the dead and if that was true why didn't they kill him why didn't they put a stop to his suffering? Why should he be a prisoner? He had committed no crime. What right had they to keep him? What possible reason could they have to be so inhuman to him?

Why? why? why?

And then suddenly he saw. He had a vision of himself as a new kind of Christ as a man who carries within himself all the seeds of a new order of things. He was the new messiah of the battlefields saying to people as I am so shall you be. For he had seen the future he had tasted it and now he was living it. He had seen the airplanes flying in the sky he had seen the skies of the future filled with them black with them and now he saw the horror beneath. He saw a world of lovers forever parted of dreams never consummated of plans that never turned into reality. He saw a world of dead fathers and crippled brothers and crazy screaming sons. He saw a world of armless mothers clasping headless babies to their breasts trying to scream out their grief from throats that were cancerous with gas. He saw starved cities black and cold and motionless and the only things in this whole dead terrible world that made a move or a sound were the airplanes that blackened the sky and far off against the horizon the thunder of the big guns and the puffs that rose from barren tortured earth when their shells exploded.

That was it he had it he understood it now he had told them his secret and in denying him they had told him theirs.

He was the future he was a perfect picture of the future and they were afraid to let anyone see what the future was like. Already they were looking ahead they were figuring the future and somewhere in the future they saw war. To fight that war they would need men and if men saw the future they wouldn't fight. So they were masking the future they were keeping the future a soft quiet deadly secret. They knew that if all the little people all the little guys saw the future they would begin to ask questions. They would ask questions and they would find answers and they would say to the guys who wanted them to fight they would say you lying thieving sons-of-bitches we won't fight we won't be dead we will live we are the world we are the future and we will not let you butcher us no matter what you say no matter what speeches you make no matter what slogans you write. Remember it well we we we are the world we are what makes it go round we make bread and cloth and guns we are the hub of the wheel and the spokes and the wheel itself without us you would be hungry naked worms and we will not die. We are immortal we are the sources of life we are the lowly despicable ugly people we are the great wonderful beautiful people of the world and we are sick of it we are utterly weary we are done with it forever and ever because we are the living and we will not be destroyed.

If you make a war if there are guns to be aimed if there are bullets to be fired if there are men to be killed they will not be us. They will not be us the guys who grow wheat and turn it into food the guys who make clothes and paper and houses and tiles the guys who build dams and power plants and string the long moaning high tension wires the guys who crack crude oil down into a dozen different parts who make light globes and sewing machines and shovels and automobiles and airplanes and tanks and guns oh no it will not be us who die. It will be you.

It will be you—you who urge us on to battle you who incite us against ourselves you who would have one cobbler kill another cobbler you who would have one man who works kill another man who works you who would have one human being who wants only to live kill another human being who wants only to live. Remember this. Remember this well you people who plan for war. Remember this you patriots you fierce ones you spawners of hate you inventors of slogans. Remember this as you have never remembered anything else in your lives.

We are men of peace we are men who work and we want no quarrel. But if you destroy our peace if you take away our work if you try to range us one against the other we will know what to do. If you tell us to make the world safe for democracy we will take you seriously and by god and by Christ we will make it so. We will use the guns you force upon us we will use them to defend our very lives and the menace to our lives does not lie on the other side of a nomansland that was set apart without our consent it lies within our own boundaries here and now we have seen it and we know it.

Put the guns into our hands and we will use them. Give us the slogans and we will turn them into realities. Sing the battle hymns and we will take them up where you left off. Not one not ten not ten thousand not a million not ten millions not a hundred millions but a billion two billions of us all the people of the world we will have the slogans and we will have the hymns and we will have the guns and we will use them and we will live. Make no mistake of it we will live. We will be alive and we will walk and talk and eat and sing and laugh and feel and love and bear our children in tranquillity in security in decency in peace. You plan the wars you masters of men plan the wars and point the way and we will point the gun.

Bantam Book Catalog

Here's your up-to-the-minute listing of every book currently available from Bantam.

This easy-to-use catalog is divided into categories and contains over 1400 titles by your favorite authors.

So don't delay—take advantage of this special opportunity to increase your reading pleasure.

Just send us your name and address and 25¢ (to help defray postage and handling costs).